ZIFFING

This book is a work of fiction. Names, characters, places, and incidents either are products of the author's imagination or are used fictitiously. Any resemblance to actual persons, living or dead, events, or locales is entirely coincidental.

Printed in Australia

Cover and internal design by Shawline Publishing Group Pty Ltd

First printing: August 2024

Shawline Publishing Group Pty Ltd

www.shawlinepublishing.com.au

Paperback ISBN 978-1-9231-7208-1

eBook ISBN 978-1-9231-7219-7

Hardback ISBN 978-1-9231-7230-2

Distributed by Shawline Distribution and Lightning Source Global

Shawline Publishing Group acknowledges the traditional owners of the land and pays respects to the Elders, past, present and future.

A catalogue record for this work is available from the National Library of Australia

ZIFFING

JAMES TURNER

For Dusty

CHAPTER 1

IN a newly painted weatherboard house, removed by two kilometres from the rural township of Kastany, Dolly Montague's demons returned to wreak havoc. Her parents heard her screaming and, when they ran to the hallway, found her squatting in the corner, crying, gripping her head as she rocked a little on her haunches.

They had witnessed the impact of these visitations while she slept but had little experience with her sleepwalking. With some uncertainty, they helped her up and back to bed. Her mother lay with her, comforting, and when the whimpering subsided, left her to sleep and returned to her own room.

In the morning, Dolly woke with only snippets of terror, but she remembered something of her parents' involvement – and that scared her as much as her nightmares.

In her waking hours, her bedroom was a protective bunker; its walls lined with bookshelves jammed with many works of history, literature and art. Dolly had a special scholastic bond with her father and wanted to follow in his professorial footsteps. To this end she had dreamed of doing a student exchange in Europe – a dream that had seemed to be derailed by a viral epidemic that shut down the world. The lockdowns had been eased lately, however, and Dolly was once more buoyed by the prospect of expanding her academic horizons and seeing the world. But her 'mental health' issues had become another barrier – at least in the eyes of her mother.

Dolly crept towards the kitchen.

'This has got out of hand,' she heard her mum say. 'At least when she was going to school, sure, she had some nightmares. But not like this. She had to get up early then. She had a regular pattern, structure.'

'The lockdowns are diminishing,' her father responded. 'I'm sure she will get back to normal.'

'No. I don't think that's all it is. I really don't want her to go to Europe.'

Dolly was scheduled to stay with a family in the Netherlands next year – just six months away. She had overheard angry exchanges between her parents on the subject, but this morning, she felt her father, Mark, measuring his words. Clearly, he did not want another fight.

'I really believe it will be good for her. Look, I will miss her terribly, as much as you will, but she will learn so much and she will be away, for a while, from things here that might be triggering her problems,' he offered.

Eavesdropping on previous arguments, Dolly would hear her mum accuse her dad's opinion of being selfish. That father and daughter had a special bond through their academic interests. That he wanted her to go to Europe to relive his own youth there – to mirror, report and recapture. But she held her tongue this time.

Dolly returned to her bed and lay, analysing her nightmares – and in fear of them. They had not affected her so severely before, apart from a few sleepwalking events, as she felt somewhat protected in her room. The walls were almost entirely lined with hundreds of titles. She loved books; she loved studying English, linguistics and history, as her father had. The thick buffer around the walls also contained biographies, poetry and fiction and offered some insulation from the horrors she imagined outside.

Most nights, without leaving her bed, she ran, fell, and stumbled in her early sleep, shrieking at the harmful intentions of spectres and demons. In her private fortress, Dolly was usually able to jolt herself awake and lie there until morning, fearful of dozing. On a few occasions, when attacks from the underworld were so vivid and frightening that she scrambled too quickly for waking, she would find herself in another part of the house or, on one occasion, outside!

She lay in bed late into the morning. The past night, after previous weeks of poor sleep, had left her exhausted. When she heard the front gate slam shut, she pulled herself up to the window with some effort, to see Jess marching off towards the town. It had been a cold night and she could see frosting on the trees, grass, her fence and the farm railings across the road.

Her dad had made breakfast and she could hear him washing up and slowly undertaking other chores, she knew, in the hope she would enter the kitchen and he could gently initiate a conversation about her *problems*. She avoided the kitchen and, pushing her bike across the yard, noticed him, with a concerned expression, sipping his mug of tea.

Mark and Jess were Dolly's parents. She loved each of them in different ways and bonded in different areas. With her dad, it was academia and he had been a strong supporter of her desire for a European exchange to mirror what he had done. But lately, his support was slipping. Where he had previously debated with her mother in Dolly's favour, she could see he too, was wondering if his daughter was developing serious issues that would forbid her living with a family, she did not know, in a foreign country. In desperation, Dolly either trivialised their concerns or reacted so angrily and offended, that they temporarily dropped the subject.

Once out the rear gate, Dolly rode slowly towards the wetlands, disappointed and angry with herself.

On the winding track, she was high in the bush, above the cyclical flooding upon which the trees and wildlife depended. Despite the winter cold, Dolly was wearing her usual shorts, high-top sneakers, and t-shirt. Strong legs powered the bike through soft ground towards the river. Beyond her book-insulated bedroom, Dolly would often retreat to the wetlands to hide out, recover and ruminate.

Dolly never ceased to be uplifted by the dramatic opening where, with an orchestra of birdsong, the bush revealed beautiful shallow lakes. Known as the Jippersomme Wetlands, the usual flocks of rosellas and finches were there this day and cockatoos screeched a greeting. A lone wallaby bounded through the shallow water. Ibises trod mud and ducks dived, while swans and pelicans glided by like elegant watercraft. The sun was high enough to reflect the huge eucalypts on the lake's surfaces.

The track took her to the edge of the bush, eventually, where she stopped and rested her foot on a fence rail. In a paddock, cows grazed, maintaining social distancing, living a life of permanent lockdown.

Dolly drank in the sensory experience that recent bad weather had disallowed and stared at the distant mist, wishing to view the mountains where she longed to be. She knew the smells and sounds of nature, combined with vigorous exercise, helped her settle down. A flock of noisy corellas accompanied her towards the lake. She tried to immerse herself in the natural world that she so loved, but her mind kept drifting back to the issue with her parents and her desire to get to Europe.

She was full of contradiction and irony, she knew. She enjoyed the way the weak winter sun burnt off the dew in the paddocks, creating steamy ground-mist and was fascinated by the fog that rolled down her creek on its way to the river. But at nighttime, fog and mist was where her ghosts, her witches and her demons emerged. It was fog that fuelled the worst of her nightmares. Even during the day, while she enjoyed the scene of surface mist and its creation, she pedalled to a higher track and left–before it *touched* her.

Dolly had been described as 'highly intelligent', 'wise beyond her years', but 'unstable' by her teachers. 'Bipolar' by a neighbour.

Although he had enthused originally, her father admitted now, it was unfortunate she was studying the two world wars with their mustard gas, trench warfare horrors, and the Blitz. All this right before the pandemic lockdowns, with their distance-from-home checks and curfews. The feeling of imminent apocalypse was mostly behind her now though and the line of trucks awaiting entry at the border town had long been allowed passage. But Dolly had difficulty, a therapist had told her parents, distinguishing reality from imagined horrors at the best of times and the nightmares had not dissipated.

The uneven path followed the creek to a point where it forked and, in recent months, Dolly would take the shorter left-branch alternative to town. She had not mustered the courage to take the right-hand route in a very long time – the route to where the creek met the river at the bridge on the edge of town – the scene of her most worrying experience. A dreadful secret. The source of much guilt and not a little shame.

In more innocent times, she would pause at the bridge. There, across the road, stood The Anvil, where she would stop in for a cheerful catch-up with Klaus.

Dolly had a new resolve this day. She had an angry determination to take the right fork in her life. If she was to regain an image of strength and responsibility with her parents, then first she had to find that in herself. She forged onwards to the bridge, a team of corellas marching with her overhead.

The Anvil was an old log and stone building, where business had evolved over the century, from farrier and forge to an engineering one, mostly maintaining farm equipment and steel gates. Klaus, the owner, and surrogate grandfather to Dolly and her two cousins, referred to by locals as the smithy, still performed some forging and shodding on occasion. She knew Klaus had already gone to the mountain and the clanging she could hear was, she presumed, created by her Uncle Lennie.

Beside The Anvil, a 100-year-old spreading peppercorn tree looked out of place, framed by the indigenous flora. But it protected the structure from the damaging Australian sun in summer and the howling gales of winter. It was also said to be a sacrificial anode for the white ants that might have otherwise attacked the building.

Dolly was aware the fog was creeping along the river where it wound behind The Anvil and she had determined not to look to that sinister place. But alas! She glanced. And, as if the underworld haunted, tested her day and night, a figure appeared. White-caped, it arose from the riverbank and disappeared behind The Anvil.

In her panic to escape, Dolly missed the pedal on her bike

and gashed open her ankle on the chain cog. The pain was intense and she quickly felt blood in her sock as she sped away. The pain, however, seemed to jolt some reality and she realised the white-clad figure was most likely Aurora. Not a ghost, not a demon, but someone she needed to avoid, nevertheless.

'Terrors upon terrors,' she muttered as she pedalled along Main Street. She crossed the road to avoid Kafé Kastany. A quick glance confirmed her suspicion that her mother would be seated at the window, with a mug of coffee and, what was now a regular, look of anxiety. She would see her daughter speed past and the look would darken.

Aunt Meredith, Jess's sister, worked there most days. Merry, she was called ironically, as she was anything but merry. Dour was the usual description the locals gave her.

Merry would be cleaning up after the few midmorning customers and Dolly pictured the scene as she rode towards her cousins, out along the North Creek Road. Merry would know Jess was agitated, wearing more than her newly acquired frown and rapping her fingers on the table. Despite her aversion to personal matters, Merry would know she was expected to join her sister at the window and listen. They were not close as siblings and seemed polarised in most areas – even their appearance. Merry was tall, dark, gaunt, and solemn; Jess was blonde, shorter, slightly curvier and, until recently, usually smiling.

Merry was under no illusion her sister had moved to Kastany to support her after her marriage breakup. Jess had to quit her job and Mark left behind a professorship to take up the lesser role of a high school teacher. Merry knew it was to avoid the harsher metropolitan pandemic restrictions to some extent, but moreover, to obtain some quietude for their misfit daughter. She brought two coffees to the table and got a cardboard tray of cakes from behind the counter.

'Here, these are yesterday's. Take them home for Mark. He likes them.'

'Thanks. I might take them as a peace offering. We had a fight this morning, or during the night, rather.'

Merry lifted her mug and replied, 'Oh. Nothing serious, I hope?' Jess weighed her sister's words for authenticity. She had left her more sympathetic and understanding friends behind in the city. In a small place like this, her cynical sister was all she had.

'Dolly is registered for this student exchange to the Netherlands next year, as you know. I don't want her to go. It's a constant source of quarrelling and I don't believe she is telling us everything, or the full extent of her problems.'

She discussed the 'night terrors' with a little reluctance, as she found Merry too often critical of Dolly. But the latter surprised her by saying, 'I am really grateful for the tutoring that she has done for both the kids. They're doing really well because of her.'

'Oh, she loves doing it. She really wants to be a teacher like her father. She loves academia; she's cut out for it. But then she excels in all of her work, which is why she wants to go to Europe. To *develop*, as she says.' *That and the superior ski-training*, Jess thought, but hesitated to add. She wondered if Merry resented the fact that Dolly went to a private school, where she got the better education and was able to enter the Interschools Ski Competition.

'Klaus has gone,' said Merry. 'I'm taking the kids up tomorrow morning.'

'Good. I am demanding that we go tomorrow as well.' It was a week before the interschools and Jess wanted Dolly to get some practice in. 'That will make her happy and, more importantly, it's a change of scenery.'

'I do hope they have grown up a bit, though. I don't want the police coming to the lodge again, like the other time.'

Jess pondered the fact that Dolly was such a contradiction; she had numerous fears and phobias but was capable of performing dangerous and illicit pranks – especially when she was with *those other two*.

While Jess resented having to play the diplomat game with her own sibling, she started by asking how Merry and the kids were coping. Emotionless as she was, Merry took it as a financial question.

'We're okay. I only get part-time here, but Lennie pays child support.'

'But the kids, they're coping with the separation?'

'Yeah, they're fine,' Merry answered, sounding as if it might be a silly question. 'Carl is with Lennie a lot... went to work with him today. Maggie sees him a bit.' Merry looked uncomfortable with anything that might lead to a discussion of *emotions*. 'Be good to get away from here for a while, though, kids need a change. Klaus has arranged work for me at the Froster.'

'I saw Carl at The Anvil, as I went past. Helping his dad. Grinding metal,' said Jess. *Carl standing recklessly in the path of flying sparks*, she thought, but did not say. *The sparks that would one day start a bushfire*, according to Mark.

'Yes, he seems to spend more time with his dad now than when we were married.' Merry paused in thought for a moment, then asked, 'Anyone else there?'

'Not that I could see.' Jess thought it a strange question, as the other cocked her head, attempting to peer obliquely at The Anvil.

***

Dolly would usually stop at the second-hand shop to peruse the basket of used books for a new title, but this time, anxiously, she fled straight past. She pedalled hard along the gravel road out to her cousins' place. En route, she recalled the previous night's parasomnia.

In her nightmare, mustard gas was a foggy virus, seeping down through Europe and Asia, killing millions of people. She had scrambled from her bed to get to higher ground. In the hallway, she had looked at the Clarice Beckett prints on the wall and screamed – the mist infusing Beckett's scenes had become gas. It had arrived in Australia! Too late to get to higher ground. She had reeled back from the prints and wailed until her parents came and led her back to bed. She thought she remembered her mum wiping her forehead with a damp cloth and uttering comfort.

Near the top of the road Dolly was aware of the proximity of the river to her right, which had wound back on itself. The river that flowed to the bridge – the bridge beside The Anvil where Aurora had just appeared and where the fog, most mornings, shrouded the memory of her terrible secret.

She stopped at a tree, just short of her destination, looking to ascertain that the neighbour's dog, Neddy, a cross between a German shepherd and something like a great Dane, was not in view. Or, more importantly, not barking. Among other things, she suffered from a form of misophonia – a panicked reaction to certain sounds. Hers was brought on by dog barking. On more than one occasion, it had caused her to get on her bike and leave. Although a cacophony of cockatoos screeched a warning and a loutish gang of magpies chortled in amusement, Dolly decided the coast was clear, and let herself into the house, calling out to her cousins.

Maggie sat at her desk, poised with a straight back and business-like attentiveness to her task. Her hair was groomed and tied in a neat ponytail. Her white shirt and beige jeans were new, clean, and pressed. Dolly winced, remembering their grandmother's *feminine and lady-like* description.

On the odd occasion they visited Grandma. She had failed to hide her disapproval of Dolly, who had recently dyed her hair from brown to a red/auburn colour and shaved the sides. She had taken up Aussie Rules Football but had only been able to play a few games between lockdowns.

'Where's Carl?' Dolly asked.

'Dad's managing The Anvil. Took Carl to work with him today. Klaus has gone up the mountain.' Maggie raised her gaze to invisible mountains in the distance.

'I was hoping you'd both be here. We've got business to sort out.'

Maggie had opened her laptop.

'Speaking of Carl, I hate to admit it, but his on-the-ground sales, through school and at footy, are booming. Almost matching mine online.'

'Did you know Carl injured one of The Bandits when we played Goonung, and got into a fight?' Dolly asked her cousin, whose look said she couldn't care less.

'We'll have them to contend with up on the mountain, as if we didn't have enough to worry about,' Dolly added.

Carl played in the boys' team for the same club as Dolly and was known around the district as *the grinning larrikin*. He would charge through packs of players, injuring himself and others, in what his dad called kamikaze-style offensives. His headmaster referred to him as 'The Temerarious Terror'.

Maggie had the same curtness and sharp tongue as her mother and, while she and her brother were different in so many ways, she had his same fearlessness.

She showed Dolly the spreadsheet.

'Look! Those two surf shops in Sydney are averaging

around forty a week, mostly to skateboarders. The ski shops in Melbourne did a hundred last week,' she said. 'But look at this! Carl sold nearly eighty!'

'That's amazing,' Dolly responded. 'Well done, Carl.'

'There's a bag of cash under the bed,' said Maggie, then continued more assertively, 'The second item of business: WitchRings.'

Dolly cut her off. 'I told you we're not doing that anymore. It's closed.'

'It's not closed! I have sent out three more invoices. And we have to pay Klaus and Carl, and I have a say in it.'

'Are you crazy?' Dolly said, 'We have to wipe our hands and get as far away from that as possible.'

Dolly could see Maggie had no intention of complying or listening to reason.

'I saw Aurora,' Dolly added, 'coming up the riverbank, near The Anvil. She wouldn't go in there, would she? She wouldn't talk to your dad? She is scaring me now.'

Maggie laughed.

'If she goes in there, Carl will hit her with a blunt instrument – or a sharp one. He'll probably do time for *bitch slaughter*.'

'That's all we need. Maggie, we've done the wrong thing. This is bad.'

'Oh, drop it, will you? It's nothing. It'll be perfectly fine.'

'No. It's fraud. It's very wrong and she's blackmailing us.'

'Well, I'm not interested. Drop it. We made good money out of it. Once I've sent the last invoices and get paid, I can transfer Aurora her share. We can forget about it.'

'I don't think she will let us. She said she wants to expand, or else!'

Maggie would not back down. She looked up to her cousin in many areas but, when she was combative, she had a battle-hardened general's non-emotive determination.

With no resolution, Dolly took the bag of money, put it in her bike basket, and rode off. She was angrily mulling over the argument when she spotted her mother leaving the café. She wanted to avoid her for the time being, so quickly turned the corner and sped off home to her room, forgetting to go to the bank.

Apart from books, there was barely enough space in the room for her single bed and wardrobe. The bookcases arched at one point to allow a small dresser with a mirror. Stuck to it were photos of her and her cousins, skiing, along with pictures of the Netherlands and Norway – places she had never been, but desperate to experience.

Dolly had not slept properly for months and hardly at all during the past week. The fresh air and hard riding had tired her sufficiently. Insulated from the outside and with the winter sun lighting her room, just enough to forbid any possibility of 'nighttime', like a chunk of glacier calving off into the ocean and drifting away, she let herself slide into a deep coma.

CHAPTER 2

THE snowboarder known as Barker waited near the top of Bulldog Run with two of his gang members. They called themselves The Bandits. Dean Kilmartin took off down Bulldog Run one more time, intending to entertain his friends from Baden College with more from his repertoire of snowboard skills. He avoided the Half Pipe this time, displaying a '360' off the rail, then headed for the big jump.

His school mates watched on; most wearing the latest argyle-patterned jackets and all sporting trendy Ziffer neck gaiters – black with the distinctive white, icicle-styled 'Z'. They did not notice the three other boarders, clad entirely in black, their faces covered, flying down from the high side. They did not notice, that is, until it was too late.

Dean had accidentally cut off one of the three on a previous run. When they hit Bulldog, Barker peeled off towards the village trail, not joining in the attack, but turned and watched the other two converge on Dean as he hit the jump.

The assault was swift and brutal.

A punch to the side of the head sent him cartwheeling off

the jump. He bounced a few times, then slid to the boundary fence that shielded the dangerous valley below. Dean's helmet prevented a serious head injury, but a loud crack was heard when his collar bone snapped as he was lodged under the bottom rail.

One Bandit yelled, 'That'll teach you to drop in on me, Dickhead.'

The attack occurred a long way before the bottom of the run so there were no lift attendants or other mountain officials to witness it. The assailants were not unobserved, however. Chairlift passengers gasped and yelled, horrified, as the gang escaped across to Heartbreak Run and down to a secluded spot at the lower side of the village. Barker ushered the other two behind buildings where they could not be seen. They removed their snowboards and trudged quickly towards their lodgings before the alarm was phoned through.

As they passed the Den, which housed the team of huskies, one of the dogs snarled uncustomarily, baring its teeth through a gap in the gate, as if sensing the evil passing by. One of the boarders – the one who landed the damaging punch – compressed a snowball in his mitt and threw it at the huskie.

'Okay, that's not necessary,' said Barker, 'they're not hurting anyone.'

***

Merry had gone into Café Froster for the informal job interview that Klaus had arranged. She left her sixteen-year-old daughter, Maggie, and fifteen-year-old son, Carl, to warm themselves by the fire in the village square.

'I don't know why we can't ski,' said Carl.

Happy skiers clomped up the granite steps from the square, laughing and chattering on their way to the chairlift.

'Mum doesn't want to pay for the weekly ticket until tomorrow. There's only an hour left today,' Maggie responded.

'Well, I'm bored now. How long has she been in there?'

The village sat on a saddle between surrounding hills; the horn of which was the Summit, and Chamounix Peak, the cantle. It was not well placed for sunshine but was more protected from blizzards and it did see good moonlight when possible.

Maggie and Carl threw twigs into the fire. They had wandered around and reacquainted themselves with all corners of the village. An abundance of snow beckoned. Beside Café Froster, were two other buildings, an information/transport office, and a bank agency, before the track turned upwards, bearing a general store, apartment buildings and lodges.

In one corner of the square was The Jagg Hotel, where Klaus waited patiently at the bar to order a tankard of ale. Eddie, the barman and owner, was confronted by three young patrons ordering a schooner of beer each. Barker looked like he could be eighteen, but the other two appeared to be underage. The barman was fairly sure the IDs they produced were false, but he detected no nervousness in their faces. He figured they were either genuine or were well practiced in their deception.

Eddie knew who the boys were connected to and where they were from. He did not want to make enemies. There was no one around who would question his responsible serving of alcohol, so he filled three schooners.

'The usual, Eddie,' said Klaus, smiling as he watched the Bandits climb the stairs to the balcony where they took up seats overlooking the square.

Eddie had worked hard to establish his business until the lockdowns had almost bankrupted him. There was a bumper crop of snow this year, however, and skiers had returned to patronise his cosy little pub, whose menu was well regarded.

Many Aboriginal artworks adorned the walls, gifts from his Wiradjuri people. Above the dining area was a large three metre by two metre abstract painting that drew praise from all who saw it. It was not abstract to Eddie, however. The painting was a gift from a lover and, for reasons unknown even to himself, he had decided not to reveal the large bogong moth that he could make out – and its meaning.

'The morons are here,' said Carl, nudging his sister.

'They must have done something. That's the only time they discard the black gear and wear the coloured jackets and white scarves,' said Maggie.

At that moment, the medical patrol snowmobile came around the bottom of Heartbreak, towing the stretcher sled and pulled up at the medical centre. The patrollers carefully carried the stretcher inside bearing the badly injured youth.

One of the three perpetrators up on the balcony stood, pointed to the stretcher, then pointed to Carl, leering, making no mistake about his intentions. Klaus had come out with his drink and took up a chair on the wooden verandah right below the Bandits. He took a sip and smiled over at his grandkids. He never looked happier than when he was at the snow. He was a huge, robust man, with a large bald head. Although he would have been able to grab all three above him with one arm and not spill a drop of ale, he was unaware of their crime, or the threat to his grandkids.

Carl and Maggie had had a few runins with the Bandits in previous seasons and were generally unafraid. But Maggie realised she would be much more comfortable if Dolly was with them for support. Brother and sister just smiled, however, and stared up at their antagonists.

Barker leant forward onto the railing and gazed off to the remote slopes and further peaks. He had intense hazel eyes and his tall, athletic frame was capped with a mop of blonde curls. With his mind elsewhere, he ignored the chatter of the other two.

'Did you know that Australia has more snow than Switzerland?' he asked them.

'Sounds like bull to me. How would they measure it?' asked Glenn, one of his offsiders

'Aerial photographs, I s'pose.'

'But how do they know how deep?'

'They can work that out.'

'How do they know what's manmade? I bet they don't even have to *make* snow over there. Manmade snow should be coloured orange or purple, so the Switzers would know if they win.'

Glenn turned and addressed his leader. 'What do you reckon, Barks?'

But he received a *you moron* look from the alpha male.

The police station was adjacent to the medical centre and Jagg's balcony was not in view from there. The policeman, Taffy Jones, began questioning the boys who had witnessed the attack. As they answered him, they looked around the square, hoping to sight three black-clad suspects, but none were evident.

As Merry descended the few steps from Froster, Taffy called out and waved. He took a step in her direction, then checked himself, and returned to his duty. Maggie looked from the cop to the Bandits. But they were unmoved, confident in their renovated appearance.

Klaus drained his tankard and joined Merry, Carl and

Maggie for the walk back to their lodge. Leaving the square, Carl looked back at the Bandits, who stood and raised their schooners.

Chapter 3

Dolly stubbornly refused to get out of the car. They had waited so long and driven so far; she was so close to her goal, yet her mum and dad had decided to stop at the bottom of the mountain and visit The Environment Centre.

'Are you doing this to punish me for something?' she yelled out the window to her parents, who were negotiating the boardwalk to *The Envy*, as they called it.

'We won't take long. Just talking to Marje. We are doing it now because it's open. They might not be open on our way home,' Jess yelled back at her pouting, recalcitrant daughter. 'Which I told you! Don't be a princess, get out, and come.'

The snow-covered peaks, that Dolly had dreamed of for so long, were all in front of her. They say you can't smell snow but Dolly was convinced she could. In her mind she could even *taste* it in the air, not long after they left the Murray River.

With her elbow out the window, she viewed with fury, the door closing at the end of the boardwalk. She liked Marje as much as her parents did, and she shared their environmental concerns, she thought, but there was a time and a place!

Behind The Envy was a vast swamp which was a maze of islands, grasses and native trees. It was a haven for water birds and was fed by a disturbingly fast-flowing creek that rushed under the boardwalk. Disturbing because, as Dolly was aware, it was fed by snow-melt. She knew good or bad snow conditions could change weekly at nature's discretion and, from the look of the creek, was diminishing all the while she sat there.

'Paradise dissolving,' she muttered as a camouflage-painted four-wheel-drive left the road at speed and skidded to a stop in the gravel behind her. A wildlife officer jumped out carrying a shotgun and ran onto the boardwalk.

'Lizzy!' Dolly yelled.

'Oh, hi, Dolly,' Lizzy answered over her shoulder. The gun and Lizzy's arm were covered in mud, which splotched on the boardwalk as she ran. 'They're shooting shovelers! Those bastards! Can you believe it?'

Dolly chased after her. She knew the shovelers: the men who worked on the mountain road, scooping and shaping snow that the graders or snow-ploughs could not get to.

Dolly's hand was trembling, she noticed, catching the door before it slammed shut behind Lizzy; she felt more wartime terror falling in on her. She recalled the shovelers were all nice fellows, always smiled and waved. She pictured now, their bloodied, bullet-ridden bodies, prostrate in the snow.

Lizzy repeated her declaration, 'They *shot* shovelers!' startling the other three inside.

Dolly could feel her gait weakening and the start of dizziness. The world inside her head had become a fearful place. As her studies became more intensified and stories of teenage soldiers being shot and gassed in muddy fields, innocent people all over Europe bombed; stories that morphed in her sleep with pandemic curfews, lockdowns, border crossings in dispute, and deaths. Dolly looked at her dad, who was running his finger down a wall chart.

'I thought the season was over and they're very distinctive. Can't tell me it was a mistake,' he declared.

It seemed that shovelers were ducks! The blue-winged shoveler was currently protected and, although Lizzy was obviously very upset, it was a duck, nevertheless.

'One of the shooters dropped this,' said Lizzy, holding up the shotgun. 'When I've cleaned up, I'll call the police. They will be able to trace it.'

'The shoveler is protected,' Marje added.

Dolly recovered and asked, 'Why do they shoot ducks? How can they do that?'

She imagined their horrible deaths as they slammed into the ground, or drowned in the lake, after hot lead-shot ripped into their bodies.

Jess said, 'How can anyone shoot *anything*?'

Mark saw her look sternly at him as she said it and mumbled, 'Let's not get into that argument right now.'

'Dolly! How are you?' Marje asked. 'I haven't seen you in a long time. Well, haven't seen *many* people in quite a while.'

'Hi, Marje,' Dolly responded, trying quickly to appear at ease. 'Yes, it's been a long time. I've been dying to get on the snow, but my parents don't seem too keen,' she accused.

Mark put his arm around her shoulders, laughing and said, 'Right! Well, let's hit the "frog 'n toad".'

As they were leaving, Marje said, 'Wait. I'm going up to Lizzy's office this week. Let's catch up, few drinks or something.'

'Great. Why don't you both come to the lodge for a get-together?' Jess offered.

Marje looked hesitant, however.

'We-e-ell, we were kind of hoping to include Hans. He

has been doing it really tough. No money. I've organised some government jobs for him, but he's still very gloomy, depressed.'

'Great... er, I mean, it's not great that he's suffered. But we all have a soft spot for Hans. Bring him along.'

'What about Klaus?' asked Marje, revealing the reason for her hesitation – the ongoing feud between the two men.

'Klaus can damn well put up with it. He doesn't own the lodge.'

'Okay. If you're sure. I'll let you know when we're coming.'

Jess took over the driving for the trip up the mountain and Dolly swapped places with her dad, happily taking in every aspect of the ascent from the front seat. Up until The Envy, Dolly had made good progress on her essay, but that would have to be put aside as they climbed the mountain.

Mark rummaged lightly through the mess on the back seat, trying to avoid fruit peels and raisins. He noticed Dolly's bag.

'We forgot to go across to Albury and bank your money.'

'Ah, yeah, well there's the agency on the mountain. I'll do it tomorrow.'

'What's your essay?'

'Still on Browning. Up At A Villa – Down In The City.'

'Ah, how appropriate.'

'That's what I thought. A pleasant coincidence.'

'I taught that one last year. What do you think?'

'I'm arguing with my teacher; she thinks that Browning intends for the Italian gentleman to change his mind halfway through the poem and *then* come around to preferring the countryside. I believe he was being satirical from the beginning.'

'Oh. I've always had the same angle as your teacher with this one.'

'Good. Then I know I'm right.'

Jess smiled across at Dolly, noting her daughter's expression of mature confidence.

Certain trees, bends and little waterfalls, were very familiar to Dolly; she had absorbed that scenery for so many years, since she was a toddler, looking for the first dollops – like washing blown from the line and scattered in the bush – then clumps, and then large drifts of snow, teasing the traveller with tantalising titbits of the grand show up high. In good years, total coverage before they got to the car park.

Despite her daughter's accusation, Jess was actually very keen to get on the slopes. Across the valley and up high, she got glimpses of ski runs at times and the lights of the village were coming on and beginning to flicker through the trees.

Skiing with her daughter had always given her the greatest enjoyment. *More importantly*, Jess thought, *Dolly preferred to ski with* her, *not her father*. Dad and daughter spent most of the year in that huddle of history, literature, etymology. *Was she resentful of that?* she mused. '*Am I guilty of competitiveness? Or dare I ask, envy?*'

Dolly was a source of great pride, at times. But she was also often remote, secretive, and troubled, a source of much worry. When they skied together, however, there was youthful skylarking, laughter – a sisterhood where all felt well. Jess was aware she had two more rivals, however. In recent years Dolly had formed a larrikin trio with her two cousins.

Jess determined, regardless, to get as much skiing as she might with Dolly. It had been two years and she missed it terribly. She had passed the valley where *that* incident happened some years ago. It was a few kilometres back and she did not even glance in its direction. She did not want to revisit the area, or the event. She had never revealed to anyone the full details of what happened that day and Dolly had only mentioned it once or twice in passing.

She had seen the skier hit a tree. She had assumed that others nearby were friends of his. She did not stop to check. When she heard he was found the next day, concussed and suffering hypothermia, she wondered if her desire to catch up with her family that day and continue their fun, had caused her to make the assumption that almost cost a life. Cattlemen's Valley had long ago shaken off the destruction of cloven-hooved grazers, but it still held a disturbing memory for Jessie Montague.

As they turned off the road, shovelers were sculpting a safety barrier of snow.

'Well, they're still alive,' Mark announced.

Dolly recognised a couple of them, especially the old guy, whom she had seen most years. While the young ones always waved and mouthed 'hello', the other, appearing to be about sixty, would only wink or smile subtly – nothing too demonstrative from him. In contrast to every other worker on the mountain, he wore an Akubra hat instead of a woollen beanie. His face was very weathered, had a large grey moustache and a long grey ponytail.

Their car turned very close to the old shoveler. If she'd had the window open he could have patted her arm. But his stare was of neither friendship nor threat; it was one of indeterminate intent that made Dolly a little uncomfortable. Yet another instant fear threatened to choke her. She glanced back to see that his gaze had followed them.

Some years, when they arrived, all the cars there would be merely white mounds, indicating they had been there for a while, and in good snowfalls. This year, however, there was no such coverage – worrying Dolly that the conditions might not be ideal. But the carpark was almost full.

The weekend was over, but it was possible that people had missed out on snow for too long; more were taking time away from school and work, to make the most of it. By the end of the week, buses would arrive to excrete large groups of students for interschools. Many of her competitors, however, were moneyed, Dolly thought, and would have practised on rare weekends between lockdowns.

Mark found one of the few empty spaces at the far end of the car park, a long way from the road. He stacked most of their belongings onto two toboggans that could be pulled along for easy portage. Dolly planted her skis upright in the snow, assessing them – her mother's hand-me-downs. She had complained that they were old and slow 'just like you' to her mother, but she could not have new gear unless she paid for it herself. Her father reminded her more than once that their tree-change had rendered the household *decidedly impecunious*.

While Dolly had proved to be entrepreneurial in recent times, half her money was earmarked for her exchange. The other half was reserved for further European expenses. When her mother was particularly vehement in her arguments for cancelling the Exchange, Dolly felt it was only the fact that she herself was contributing, that tipped the balance in her favour.

Waiting for the commuter van to take them from the car park to their lodge, Mark recalled Marje's words.

'Poor old Hans, eh? He's a lovely fellow despite all the war stories.'

'Yes, he is,' Dolly muttered, but her mind was selfishly off at the resort.

She wondered if Maggie and Carl had arrived early enough to ski for the afternoon. It was late. The lifts would have closed for the day and her cousins would have stowed their gear in lockers and already trudged back to the lodge.

Dolly was eager for mild, cold blasts to cleanse her of the dark thoughts and nightmares of recent times. Although she had no real friends, save for her cousins, and little interaction with her peers, she was aware that other students shared her feelings, for more than a year, of an impending Armageddon, that most adults failed to appreciate.

Before the village, where the road took a sharp left elbow to the lodges, stood Tyrol Inn: a slender four-storey wooden building the locals referred to as 'Dark Tower'. It was a very old structure, clad in vertical weatherboards, protected with Creosote, a possible carcinogen, that rendered it very dark brown, or black in places.

Dark Tower provided cheap accommodation and Aunt Merry maintained it. It was occupied only by *ne'er-do-wells* or backpackers, snowboarders, and others of suspicious origin, plotting mischief at the dingy bar within. Klaus called it, 'A mediaeval turret, stormed by the barbarians that now occupy it.'

The van slowed to take the sharp bend, a lone snowboarder juddered to a stop in the shadow of the tower, as if on cue: a tall figure in dark clothing, with a dark hood. The van turned up towards the village and Dolly bristled, feeling the boarder's sinister gaze follow her.

Dolly had heard, often enough, that she was *gifted*. But, in her mind, she was mainly *gifted* with visions of predatory assailants. With each knot and rise, Dolly was either elated or returned to her *darkness*; but then the mercury of her emotions climbed up from the valley of darkness and bathed in lights.

There was always a white Christmas feel to the village at night. A low stone wall in the village square enclosed a fire that blazed during clement weather. Some teenagers burnt long twigs and waved them about dangerously, watched by customers gathered on the deck outside Café Froster. The prancing, corroboree flames were reflected on the buildings that guarded the square.

The road had turned on itself enough to find that Dark Tower was adjacent to the village, albeit lower, with just its blackened top windows keeping watch.

'There's the Jinker,' Dolly exclaimed, joyously. Getting transport from the village was a lottery. As well as the five motorised commuters taking guests from the village square to their lodges, there was a horse and buggy. She had named it the Jinker – a title that caught on – for the jingle-jangle sound it made, despite her father insisting, pedantically, that the name applied to logging wagons.

Most people wanted to ride in the Jinker, especially children, as long as the weather was favourable. The old guy who drove it had done so for many seasons. He had a bushy, white moustache, crinkly smiling eyes and a cattleman's hat and coat. Dolly always referred to him as John Thorpe, for her own amusement, but others knew him as Cliff.

The commuter had stopped to allow a family with three excited little children, to cross the road and climb aboard the novelty horse-drawn conveyance to their lodge. A very light snowfall: its flakes fluttering, dancing and reflecting firelight, added further wonder to the scene.

The Montagues had a noisy, shuddering climb up Stirling Track to their lodge. Sitting opposite, Jess was pleased to see a relaxed, *lightness of being* had returned to her daughter.

The driver announced, 'Innsbruck! Here we are!'

CHAPTER 4

INNSBRUCK Lodge, built when the mountain was first being developed, was possibly the oldest and smallest at the resort. The exterior walls of the cellar and first floor were constructed of stones hewn from local granite; the storey above clad in weatherboards – many of them warped and cracked. The roof was of oft-repainted corrugated iron, not steep enough to avoid being a repository for large accumulations of snow.

The Lodge was owned by a membership of Klaus, Merry, the Montagues, and two other families descended from the original group that built it. Inside, it had timber lined walls and a cosiness that was so familiar and comfortable to all of them.

From the road, steps had been fashioned in the snow and smacked down ice – hard, to the entrance of the lodge. There was a luge beside the steps, finishing with an upward slope, allowing toboggans of luggage to slide to a gentle stop at the door.

Along the road and across the slope from Innsbruck, a number of lodges were visible, scattered through the trees. While the driver handed luggage and gear to Dolly and her dad, Jess stood, taking in the beauty of the snow gums – their variety of shapes and colours, and their decorations of snow and ice.

'They're here!' Maggie shouted, running from the lodge with Carl close behind. They made their way carefully up the slippery steps to help with the luggage. There were cheerful greetings and hugs between cousins, as if they had not seen each other in a long time – such was their joy at being together at the snow.

Maggie asked Dolly about her trip up.

'I'll tell you when we get inside,' Dolly replied. 'Did you ski today?'

'No. We got here too late. Mum wouldn't pay for half-day lift tickets.'

Maggie and Carl grabbed some luggage while Dolly received her ski gear from the driver. As Maggie got to the luge, however, Carl hit her behind the knees with the toboggan. She fell forward, plummeting down the slide, screeching, and slammed into luggage at the bottom.

'I'll kill you!' she screamed up at him, but when she tried in fury to scramble up the path, her feet slipped from under her again and she fell face-down.

Merry had seen this from the window and yelled, 'Carl, that's the last straw. I've had it with you. You're going back on the bus tomorrow to stay with your father.'

Inside the entrance, the small foyer had a wooden bench-seat along one wall and a flagstone floor with centre grate for knocking mud and snow off outdoor boots. There were three doors: one led into the lodge, one to a storage room for skis, poles, toboggans, etc, which was not much bigger than a wardrobe, and similarly small, the third was the drying room, where wet gear dried overnight.

Carl threw his boots into the drying room, singing, 'The

wheels on the bus go round and round, round and round, round and–' Klaus appeared in the doorway and playfully grabbed him by the throat.

'Ah, mein wunderkind,' he announced as Dolly entered.

Klaus loved his grandchildren. With Dolly, his favouritism of her was often thinly veiled.

'Hi, Grandpa,' answered Dolly, grinning, and embracing him warmly.

Inside the lodge was a small, cosy lounge room, a kitchen, two small bathrooms and five very small bedrooms with a double bunk in each. They all took up seats in the small lounge room, with its wood-fire blazing and Dolly took in the familiar and comfortable ambience. Klaus pointed to each of the kids and issued his stern warning, 'Now, I don't want any trouble this year. I don't want police or mountain staff knocking on the door.'

This invoked sardonic looks from Mark and Jess, as Klaus seemed to encourage, or at the least, find amusement in their shenanigans. Klaus was managing the lodge for a month, with some help from Merry, then one or both of the other families would take over.

'Don't worry,' said Merry. 'Carl is going home on the bus tomorrow.'

'Good. That's one less I have to worry about.'

'And the other two have been warned,' she added.

Mark and Jess settled near the open fire in the lounge, while Klaus poured each a glass of wine. Merry declined the offer to join them and busied herself in the kitchen, located on a mezzanine behind the fireplace – or *pretended* to be busy, as Jess often felt.

One wall was almost entirely of glass, with a door leading out onto a wide balcony, looking out over snow gums to further alpine peaks.

Klaus had a booming voice that matched his stature and when he bellowed 'Ziffers! Come here!' the command could be heard throughout the lodge.

Dolly was in good spirits, initially; laughing and boisterous with her two partners. She called an impromptu business meeting in her room, expecting some conflict, but the light snow falling outside her window invoked a more peaceful mood, suddenly. So she waivered and decided to keep her powder dry. They agreed to reconvene the following evening and to ask Klaus, in the meantime, to put their money in his safe.

One of Dolly's many preoccupations was to renovate old words – or invent completely new ones. As such, she had decided that the word *ziff* would mean *to ski very fast* – and the gang of three called themselves *the Ziffers*. Mountain staff knew *the Ziffers* as troublemakers, akin to other occasional 'nuisance gangs' at the resort.

'See that broken handrail on the balcony?' Klaus asked, 'That's from a pile of snow that came off the roof, the size of a Volkswagen. I gotta fix it tomorrow. Be careful out there. Don't forget Tom Farrell.'

He was constantly reminding them of the hazard of snow falling from the eaves. The story was that Tom Farrell, one of the original members who built the lodge, was found dead one morning outside the cellar door, under a pile of snow. The version that Márk and Jess had heard from others was that Tom was extremely intoxicated and died of hypothermia, long before the snow fell. They let Klaus tell his version, however, as snow coming off the roof was a very real danger.

The lodge was originally named 'Misof'. Misof being an acronym of the surnames of the original members. Dolly and her father lobbied to have the name changed and, when she informed that the locals often replaced the 'M' with a 'P', she achieved agreement.

Darkness began to creep in, and the evening was getting colder. A breeze came up the valley, rustling the trees and causing the light snow to fluff around as it fell. Below Innsbruck's balcony, through the trees, were two lodges before the slope overlooking Sunset Run and a large, dark valley called The Cauldron, whence the worst southerly weather boiled. At the end of the balcony Maggie pointed to a flat spot beside the lodge.

'That's where Charlotte will be,' she announced, unloading the contents of her backpack for Dolly's inspection. She pulled out a large hat with a colourful band, that would not be out of place at the Melbourne Cup. She had also purchased, from the second-hand shop, a large orange jacket, a handbag and a scarf.

Carl suggested they go and get shovels from the cellar and start immediate construction of their traditional snowwoman.

'I'll meet you outside,' Dolly said, and her mother repeated Klaus' warning to 'stay away from the eaves'.

'No. We need firewood,' Klaus interrupted, 'Go to the cellar. You can all help get wood. Thanks.'

Klaus had always told the kids that Tom Farrell's ghost loitered in the darkness beneath the lodge. Behind the drinks bar at one end of the lounge, was a trapdoor that led to the cellar, often called *Tom's Bedroom*.

Dolly took a quick deep breath and tried to adopt a nonchalant gait towards the bar. Her cousins scampered down the ladder, but Dolly hesitated, sitting at the top, peering down into the fearful gloom. The dark cellar had housed fear and horrors for her in previous years, she thought, but *now*... after her problems had become much worse. She determined to descend slowly and tentatively after Carl found the battery-operated lantern that cast a barely adequate light over the pile of firewood.

To Dolly, the cellar felt like a burial crypt that amplified the painful groans of the old timbers tortured above. The flimsy door, leading to the outside, allowed thin cracks of light in the wrong places. And the whisperings of cold.

Descending the ladder with trepidation, Dolly was close to the bottom when Klaus closed the trapdoor to stop the cold rising into the lodge. Dolly froze, willing her eyes to get used to the semi-darkness, wanting to be back in her bedroom. She felt chilled whisperings from dark corners and Tom Farrell's cold breath on the back of her neck. Dolly could hear Carl rattling shovels in a dark corner, while Maggie gathered firewood. She felt immersed in the blackness of fear, and climbed slowly, backwards, up the ladder. She pushed up the trap door and sat at the top, breathing heavily.

She gathered strength and descended again, still with some trepidation.

In the lounge room, Dolly's parents waited until the trapdoor was closed again before continuing the discussion of their concerns about their daughter.

'Don't let her near the weird Dutchie, then,' Klaus suggested.

'That's very rude,' Jess quickly responded. 'Hans is a very nice fellow. He means well, and apparently he's been doing it tough.'

'Yeah, we all have,' said Klaus. 'I have no truck with his whingeing.'

'You can be insensitive.'

'Well, I'm being protective of my little mate. How did she handle the schoolwork, anyway?'

'Extremely well. She's an intelligent girl. She always gets good marks. Especially history and literature.'

'I'm now teaching her a bit of Latin on the side,' Mark put in, proudly, 'She loves language.'

'Well, she's a real entrepreneur.' Klaus said, then added, 'The online business.'

'They are *all* involved in that,' Merry interposed.

Klaus concurred and offered that they had also made him a bit of money on the side.

'Oh, yes. The *ring things*. What happened with that?' Jess asked, 'Haven't heard them mentioned in a while.'

'The WitchRings? Nah, well, it's all finished, had its day. A good earner for a little while, though.'

'We've issued warnings about the Ziffer activities. Hopefully they've grown up a bit. However, I do want Dolly to let her hair down, have some fun. We've been very concerned about her.'

'Really?' Klaus seemed surprised. 'I've seen a lot of her and she seems fine to me.'

'You do all the fun things with her. You're not there when the darkness and fog roll in.'

Klaus looked nonplussed. It was the first time he had heard of any real problems.

Jess added, looking from Merry to Klaus, 'I know you think she was always a bit strange, as everyone else does.'

'Eccentric and interesting,' Klaus interrupted, smiling.

'She refuses to talk about it, saying it's nothing, but we hear the screams, witness the visitations, the nightmares, live with her paranoia.' Mark added.

'She seems hesitant to go out when it's foggy. She denies it, but we see. On two very foggy nights we heard her, in her sleep, yelling "*Gas mask! Where's my gas mask!*"' said Jess.

Mark added again, 'Another time she yelled *Can you hear*

them? Can you hear them? Up there! Hide! Then sobbing and strange murmurings.'

'She has nightmares most nights. We know, but she denies it. She appears very nervy lately,' said Jess.

'And, unlike the school where I teach, hers has students from both sides of the border, so, with the ever-changing rules, they were given the option of home-schooling if they wanted,' said Mark. 'Of course she opted to stay at home, becoming more and more isolated.'

'She didn't really have friends, anyway,' Merry contributed, getting an offended "*trust you to be rude*" look from her sister.

'Sssshhh,' warned Klaus, putting a finger to his lips. There was another entrance to the cellar, if you were small enough – the wood box next to the fireplace. Dolly's head appeared to be sitting in the bottom of the box when the door slid open. She smiled at the adults sitting about and stacked wood, passed to her by her cousin.

After a lot of grunting and sighing, Dolly had stacked sufficient wood and, before closing the door, asked, 'Why are we adding to global warming, burning all this wood?'

'We love the ambience of flame,' Jess responded to the head disappearing through the floor. 'Is it environmental concern or laziness fuelling your question?'

Descending, once again, into the poorly lit cellar, for Dolly, there were dark corners where anything could be hiding. There were discarded, broken tools and paraphernalia that had not been cleaned up in years.

The cellar was a hand-dug excavation under the lodge. It had an earthen floor and a rudimentary attempt had been made, at times, to fashion low walls with the rocks left over from construction of the building above.

Above the pile of firewood hung a modern chainsaw, but its dead predecessor lay nearby – a very large model, no longer produced. Now heavily rusted, it had been lying there in the dirt since they could remember.

'You got the shovels?' Dolly asked. 'We'll make the toboggan run after Charlotte.'

They did not need to climb back up; there was a rickety old door that opened, where Tom Farrell expired, below the balcony. When they opened the door to throw the shovels out into the snow, light from a lodge below lit up a little more of the cellar. Dolly could see strange, unidentified shapes, an antique toboggan, and a rusty, one-legged wheelbarrow.

It had started to snow outside and a breeze came up from the valley, rattling the flimsy wooden door and blowing snowflakes into the cellar. While the girls created the snowwoman, Carl was charged with building the curved luge for their nighttime tobogganing, with strict instructions for a higher wall on the curves, to avoid injury.

While they worked, Maggie asked Dolly, 'Hey, can I bunk in with you? I don't want to share with Mum, especially if we want to sneak out sometimes.'

Dolly hesitated a little too long before agreeing. She knew it was a practical idea, but she wondered how much *night terror* Maggie would witness. If Maggie needed some hint that something was wrong, she only needed to observe Dolly stop digging every now and then and look about, uncomfortably. She would appear worried, at times shaking slightly. Maggie had little doubt that her cousin did not want to be anywhere outside at night.

***

Just below the village, the Jinker was delivering its two passengers, a man and a woman, to their lodge. The scene could not have been more romantic; they were rugged up and nestled together atop a horse-drawn carriage. Moonlight illuminated the snowflakes that fluttered and danced around, landing on their shoulders.

Cliff heard the thwack as the snowball exploded against the horse's neck. It reared and jumped sideways, pushing his partner off the track. She neighed in fright as she scrambled to gain her footing on the soft slope. Two legs went off the track. The carriage lurched sideways and might have rolled down the hill, potentially killing its passengers, if it had not jammed against a tree. Cliff could see three dark figures stick snowboards under their arms and disappear over the top ridge.

'Hey! You bastar–' was all he could yell before being thrown off. He tumbled a little before he jumped to his feet and continued to yell after the assassins.

The woman in the Jinker screamed hysterically. The carriage was buffeted against the tree as the horses struggled to regain their footing. If it lost the support of the tree, it would tumble and roll down the hill, taking all with it. The male passenger yelled in pain. His arm was jammed between the tree and the Jinker; his partner on top of him screaming. The commotion brought people from nearby lodges and onto balconies nearby.

Cliff scrambled in the soft snow, trying to grab the mare's harness; to sooth her and guide her back onto the trail. He risked a stomping as she danced around in a panic, trying to get a foothold on the angle. The passengers held on to avoid sliding out, all the time yelling and bellowing. The horse limped and struggled, appearing to be badly injured.

Cliff could no longer see the boarders, but continued, 'Hey, you there... STOP! Stop them!'

CHAPTER 5

EVERY morning of the season, Hans Schulklapper opens his second-storey window, looks out over the village square, and the hills beyond, assessing the condition of the snow. He lives above his little ski-hire shop, humbler than the others on the mountain. Assessing the conditions is moot because he rings the bell anyway. The large brass bell hangs under the eave of his building where he can reach the donger-rope from his window.

Hans clangs the donger back and forth every morning at 8.00 am. The resounding noise bounces off surrounding peaks, buildings, and valley walls, waking everyone – calling snow-worshippers to join the chairlift queue – but hopefully after they have visited his shop to hire equipment.

Occasionally, if it is low light, he will see Winston, the village wombat, waddling home late to bed, leaving a trail of his small footprints across the square. The bell is a sure signal to Winston that annoying humans are about to emerge in large numbers.

The Ziffers had loaded the dishwasher, cleaned the bathrooms, and vacuumed. They were clicking into their skis under the balcony when they heard the bell. They then skied carefully between the trees and two lodges, stopping at the lip of the steep drop-off that would give them access down onto Sunset Run. Paused at the lip, Dolly was aware they had not skied for a long time and things should be taken carefully at the start. Even the reckless Carl had hesitated.

Jess yelled a cheerful warning as she, Merry, and Mark were leaving the lodge. Merry was off to start work at the Café Froster and the other two would walk with her, carrying their skis. Merry carried a black bag, full of money. As they trod carefully down the icy road to the village, Merry complained that Klaus' idea of managing the lodge simply involved playing loud, classical music up in his room, while she did most of the work.

'And, at The Anvil, he apparently spends all day welding his sculptures, while Lennie does all the hard work,' she added, in a rare voice of support for her ex-husband. It was common knowledge that Klaus fancied himself as a great conductor and an artist, and, had his parents not brought him to this *uncultured* country, he would have been *something*. Yet here he was, forced to make a living in work that was beneath him.

The Ziffers tackled the steep drop and joined Sunset at high speed without incident. Sunset would take them to Boomerang Run, at the bottom of which they would catch the Cannonball Chairlift to other runs to get up to the village.

The liftie greeted them with, 'Ah, my first customers. Good morning guys.' He was older than other lifties, with a mixed Celtic accent, Dolly observed, enhanced by an Irish Rovers song playing at his lift station.

'Good morning,' Maggie beamed. With excited chatter, the grinning Dolly and Carl revealed the thrall of their first ski in two years.

'Take your backpacks off,' the liftie warned, as the chair

came around, scooped them up and commenced its dangling ride up the valley. It was a clear, sunny morning; little icicles glinting and melting from trees.

'Look! There's Winston's tracks, or one of his mates, off to bed.' Always on the lookout for wildlife, Maggie then pointed excitedly to an eagle circling in the distance. It rose out of the valley, banked, climbed higher and seemed to follow the chair for a few seconds, as if considering, then discounting, Ziffers as prey.

Maggie recognised the liftie at the top.

'Sonja! Hi!' Indicating with her thumb, as they alighted the chair.

'Maggie, Dolly, Carl.' Maroon 5 played backing as Sonja yelled, with her Scandinavian accent, 'Have a great day and stay out of trouble!'

From there they needed to take two more runs: The Schute across to Heartbeat Run and down to the village. On The Schute, they could see snowboarders practicing tricks at Half Pipe. Despite the excitement of the morning, Dolly was wary. She paused at the top of Heartbeat and cautioned the others. Buddy Holly's 'Heartbeat' was playing at the top station and, in recent years, Kelly Clarkson's 'Heartbeat' had been established at the bottom.

'Carl, that guy, Glenn, you hurt playing footie, let's not forget he was one of The Bandits. Probably still is. They will be bigger now and probably a lot meaner, especially if they have this score to settle.'

'We're not scared of them,' Maggie replied.

Dolly was often amazed at her cousin's resolve. She displayed, like her brother, a reckless abandon, at times – despite her frail and *feminine* appearance.

'Well, just be very watchful. I certainly don't want a fight if we can avoid it.'

They got down to the village just after 9.00 am and *skretssshed* to a hard stop, spraying the Yupik Ski Hire sign. Hans and his assistant, Roland, were busy fitting people with skis and boots.

'Mijn Ziffers!' he declared, ignoring customers briefly and throwing his arms around each in turn. 'I have missed you guys.'

After their greetings, Hans asked if he could rent them some gear, but Dolly lamented the fact that they could not afford anything but a locker, and would have to make do with their old hand-me-downs. From their joint funds, Maggie paid for a locker, and they stored their backpacks for the day.

Hans busied himself with customers and did not notice the three Bandits slip in the side exit door. The narrow space between the lockers was perfect for an ambush. The Bandits blocked the light from the window, giving themselves a darker, more ominous appearance. Dolly remembered Barker, the leader; she recognised the blonde curls, but he was now taller and more substantial. In panic, she tried to push past him but he was an immovable bollard.

'Well, it's the Sniffers,' Barker sneered at them. 'The skiers who think they're better than everyone else.'

'Look, if you're feeling inadequate,' Dolly responded brusquely, 'get some counselling, but don't bother us.'

She tried to push past again but Barker was still immovable. She then noticed that one of them was Glenn and he was staring murderously at Carl. She was trying not to reveal her fear. At the same time, she could not fathom the looks of calm, almost amusement, on the faces of Maggie and Carl. Hans also noticed what was happening then and, when she saw him move towards the confrontation, Dolly's relief was palpable in that confined space.

'It's Ziffers. We are the Ziffers,' said Carl with a look that said, *We are not backing down.*

The Bandits laughed and each of them, in turn, pulled his trendy, Ziffer neck gaiter up over his nose.

'That's pathetic,' Barker spat out at them. 'What do you do when you go surfing? Call yourselves Quicksilver or Billabong, maybe?' This got a raucous response from his mates.

At that point Dolly's smile equalled that of her cousins and she took on the same fearless demeanour. The Bandits were a little confused and disarmed by this new confidence, but Barker continued, 'You skiers are out of date. Just because you've got money, you think you own the place. But you'll be extinct soon.'

'I suppose if you're a snowboarder, you've got to act tough to cover up for the fact that you can't ski,' said Maggie, still smiling in the face of potential violence.

Barker pulled his Ziffer off his nose and stretched it out from his mouth, sneering, 'The Ziffers...'

'Yeah, means we ski very fast,' said Carl.

'When I bought this, my dad told me a *ziff* was a *beard*, and it's designed to look like you have a beard. Doesn't mean *fast*, you morons.' Barker went on, despite the brighter grins from his opponents. 'Beard suits you girls, though, but not *baby boy* here.'

Carl just smiled. Barker could not understand why he was failing to antagonise.

'That's not quite true,' said Hans, coming up behind them. 'In German, "Ziffer", it means a figure, a number.' He points to Dolly, Maggie, and Carl in turn. 'Three in number.'

'Well, I'm not interested in any German,' Barker responded over his shoulder, then aggressively to Dolly, 'Why don't you choose an English word for your little tribe here – instead of copying trendy labels?'

'Well, our grandfather *is* German.'

'It seems we got war, then,' said Hans, trying to make light of the situation. 'Pity I don't rent out guns, maybe.'

'We don't need guns,' replied Carl, grinning. 'We can sort this out.'

He stood on his tiptoes, attempting to stare eye-to-chin with the much taller Glenn. Carl had what Klaus often called 'sangfroid', which the elders often feared would land him, and the girls, in real danger.

Customers entered Yupik and Hans ushered the combatants out into the square, where he felt it would not escalate under CCTV and plenty of witnesses. Dolly noticed Barker glance up at the camera as they exited. Glenn immediately chested Carl and Maggie attempted to intervene as pre-punch jostling ensued.

'Ah, Senior Constable Jones!' Dolly shouted, waving to Taffy who was, fortuitously, having a coffee on the deck at Froster. She quickly grabbed Carl by the arm, nudging him and Maggie in that direction, while trying to think of a subject for discussion.

'Your mother's not here," he said to Maggie, 'she's gone to the bank, I think.'

Sitting without invitation, Dolly renewed their acquaintance, mentioned the weather and enquired about the policeman's health. But Taffy Jones was more observant than she gave him credit for.

'Just sitting here, sipping a coffee and considering the paperwork involved when I put a bullet into one or two of you if that altercation had resulted in manslaughter by snowboard or ski pole.'

At that moment Merry came up the steps. She was surprised to see the kids and offered them hot chocolates. The Bandits had disappeared from sight but Dolly could not be sure they weren't watching and waiting. She wanted to start her training but decided to wait. Carl and Maggie were happy to leave but agreed to wait.

'That was a strange experience,' Merry said.

'What?'

'At the bank. I felt strange, anyway, with a big bag of the kids' money. Like a Mafia boss or a drug dealer, but that woman, the teller, so unwelcoming and angry-like.'

'Beth. Yeah, she's a strange one. She's leaving shortly now that regional people can get work in the cities. She hates the cold, never wanted to be here.'

'You seem to know a lot about a furtive woman who never speaks, except for the bare, banking minimum,' said Merry, examining Taffy's profile as he took a sip from his coffee.

'My job to,' he mumbled.

When Dolly felt an appropriate time had elapsed, and they had finished their drinks, she thanked Merry and the Ziffers clomped off, carrying their skis up to the Heartbeat chair.

On the chairlift, the song soon gave way to the whirring sound of cable wheels. Perfect weather afforded them a view of lower peaks as far as they could see. The plague had stolen some of the transition towards adolescence and the Ziffers had not updated their anthem. So, for want of better, they sang to the skiers below:

Ziffing through the snow,
Downhill lightning fast,
Stop'n watch us go,
Ziffers flying past.

Dolly tried to relax, soak up the beautiful alpine environment that she had missed for so long, and to think about her style and technique, imagining her way through the slalom gates. But she kept slipping back to Barker's threats and Carl's provocation.

As they were carried past the Half Pipe, she pointed to the snowboarders.

'Carl, this isn't Westside Story or a pantomime. This is very dangerous.'

'What's Westside Story?'

'It doesn't matter, but you don't just start singing and dancing, and pretend it's not real. Those guys are much bigger now and I don't think they'll forget about us.'

'There's your parents!' Maggie exclaimed, seeing Jess and Mark skiing amongst many others onto Cannonball.

'Muuuum! Daaaad!' Dolly shouted, but was not heard. 'One advantage in having parents who wear the oldest and cheapest gear is you can always spot them,' she said to Maggie.

They made their way across to Baldy, where the interschools competition runs would be prepared in a few days' time. At that point in time, however, they were just bare runs – roped off and out-of-bounds.

They had never obeyed signs or warnings before and were not about to start. In the absence of suitable poles, Carl and Maggie positioned themselves as two gates at correct intervals and Dolly practised her technique, brushing them with her shoulder as she negotiated each. They would then all have a recreational, downhill chase, before catching the chair back to Baldy and repeating the process.

Carl and Maggie were content to help their cousin in her quest for Interschools glory and they were getting plenty of skiing along with it. By lunch time they had carved up the quarantined run on Baldy, so much that it would need a serious re-grooming.

Even as they passed the Half Pipe, and were reminded

of the danger there, Dolly was, for the present, happy and had returned to the rapture of previous years. They entered Yupik to get their lunches from their backpacks and found Mark and Jess doing the same. The ski-chatter and laughter from the Ziffers gave Dolly's parents some hope for snow-induced rehabilitation.

CHAPTER 6

KLAUS tried to hurry Dolly from the breakfast table. It was after 9.00 am. Merry had gone to Froster and the others would be already on the slopes. He was crashing and banging, cleaning the kitchen – making a show of one of the few chores for which Merry had not accepted delegation. Klaus skied when he felt like it, but this day he wanted to make drawings for new sculptures and play Franz Liszt pieces loudly.

Dolly had fought, firstly that morning with her mum, then with Maggie. Everyone had left without her. She scraped her bowl aggressively; she was dazed and sleep deprived.

The previous night, Dolly wanted to test her newfound confidence and her assumed peace of mind. So she had organised a *break-out*. Just after midnight, the Ziffers escaped, as they had so often, and walked down to the village. At a loss for what to do, that would be reckless or exciting, they skirted the buildings guarding the village square and kept out of sight.

Loud music and laughter emanated from The Jagg and from another bar opposite. A few intoxicated revellers wandered around. There was not much else going on. The Bandits were there at the fire; they seemed equally at a loss for illicit activity and, after throwing a few snowballs into the flames, and one at the window of the Medical Centre, they left. The Ziffers followed them at a distance, keeping to the shadows and watched them enter their lodgings at Dark Tower.

'There's The Turk,' Carl whispered.

The Turk looked after the huskies and ran the dog-sled tours. Apart from that, he was a loner; a thin, middle-aged, solemn man. He always wore a hoody and seemed to shun social contact. Away from the dogs, he was rarely seen, but occasionally, he had been reported skiing, off-piste or on remote slopes, alone. He could also be seen going to the bank or buying cigarettes at the general store. He led a furtive existence and the consensus was that Dark Tower was the best place for him.

He was on a balcony above the front door and seemed to strain, in the darkness, to ascertain who was below him, as the Bandits entered. Then he moved along the balcony, casting about, seeming intent on finding someone, or something.

'I heard that he's cruel – that he cut someone up in a fight, and spent time in jail,' said Carl.

Dolly hushed him and advised him quietly not to put any stock in rumour.

'He does give you the creeps, though, doesn't he?' she added.

'I wonder what The Turk is looking for,' said Maggie.

'Too often people around here are identified by their nationality,' complained Dolly. 'It's borderline racism.'

'We'll call him the Creep, then,' was Carl's solution.

'Loners are often the targets of rumour they don't deserve,' said Dolly.

Not far from Dark Tower was the Den, where the huskies were housed.

'Let's go down and see if the dogs are awake,' Maggie suggested, but Dolly refused.

Dolly liked the huskies and their howl did not cause a misophonic episode, like a barking dog. If they did bark, which was rare, it was a short and sharp howling. She pointed out that if they started howling, however, it might draw attention, and as they would need to climb up the slope from there, they would be easily seen.

'There's someone there,' Maggie exclaimed a little too loudly, 'all white, behind the Den.'

They watched the figure move behind the trees towards Dark Tower. The Turk continued to search back and forth, swaying a little, and moving his head from side to side. He then appeared to stare directly at the Ziffers. Dolly squeezed the arms of Carl and Maggie – the signal to keep perfectly still.

'He can't possibly see us,' Maggie whispered. Unconvinced, though, they remained rigid in the dark.

The Turk returned to searching the trees. But he shot a look back in the direction of the Ziffers, seeming to glare, then opened the door and left the balcony.

'I think we'd better go home,' Dolly suggested, with a sharp intake of breath, 'nothing happening.'

***

Klaus slammed cupboard doors, the noise bringing Dolly back to the present. She finished her breakfast, listening to him swear and thump. Before having to do chores that were *beneath* him, Klaus was already in a foul mood. Jess had informed him that they were having a get-together that night with Lizzy, Marje and Hans.

'They invited the bloody Dutchie,' he announced.

On any other occasion she would have fought with him over the statement, but Dolly was tired, in a bad mood herself, and she shuffled off to the drying room.

She walked to the village. There was not enough snow cover along the road, so she carted her skis on a toboggan rather than take the challenging route across Sunset and into the valley, which would have put her even further behind schedule.

Halfway up Heartbeat she could see the ski school starting up, which brought a smile to her face. It never failed to lift her spirits, looking at the laughing faces of the little ones learning to ski – their joy – their whole ski-lives ahead of them.

She skied across to Wombat Chair and alighted to the sound of Snow Patrol's 'Chasing Cars'. She cut across to Baldy, where, despite their tiff that morning, Carl and Maggie had agreed to meet her for training.

Approaching, Dolly asked, 'Did you hear? They're having a get-together tonight and Hans is coming. We don't get a chance to talk business at Yupik. We can pin him down tonight.'

'Yes, that's good. But I've got some bad news,' Maggie informed her quietly, 'Justine-from-Trinity is here. Well, she's over on Gunbarrel.'

Justine had been Dolly's most fierce rival for the gold in previous Interschools seasons. She was a very talented skier. On top of that, her parents provided her with the most expensive gear, including top-of-the-range, slalom race skis. She had skied most weekends of her winters and had professional training.

'Damn. I didn't need to hear that,' said Dolly. 'I'm going over to have a look.'

She had thought to claw back some ground in the inequity by having the week before Interschools to train but, of course, Justine-from-Trinity would have the same advantage.

'We'll come with you.' Maggie waved Carl over and motioned for him to follow.

The Ziffers jumped off Smokey Chair and made their way across to Gunbarrel. Justine was poised at the top of the run, adjusting her ski mask; her knees slightly bent, her posture straight. The cousins hid behind a clump of low snow gums, watching. To Dolly she was a lithe, athletic ballerina on skis – but that was probably just her imagination, she owned. To anyone else, Justine might have been just another young person in a red and black designer outfit.

She tried various runs and never repeated the same one twice. She had a few unsteady moments, Dolly noted, but, for the most part, Justine was smoothly ziffing. It had been a long time since anyone had been allowed to ski, but it seemed Justine had not lost her snow legs.

Skiing a parallel run, Dolly continued to observe, with some annoyance, the smoothness of Justine's style; her seemingly perfect technique, and those skis, as if motorised, seemed to be conducting the turns for her – turns that were aggressive and at uniform distances, indicating she was negotiating imaginary slalom gates. Dolly had to admit that her rival looked focused, determined, and confident.

After a while, Maggie and Carl were thoroughly bored and wanted to put an end to the surveillance.

'Watch this,' said Carl, as he took off around a group of boulders, chasing Justine.

There was no time to stop him, so Dolly and Maggie shot down the adjacent slope, watching through the line of trees as they went. Dolly panicked that Carl's antics would expose her to ridicule and accusations of stalking. But Carl's effort ended in one of his most spectacular spills ever. At the end of a spiralling, protracted tumble that threw up sprays of snow, he lay prone, with his head pointing downhill, while Justine-from-Trinity continued on, apparently unaware.

Either that, or she did not care that someone might be hurt, thought Dolly.

Maggie was through the trees swiftly to help her brother. When Dolly arrived, Carl was getting to his feet, groaning in pain, while Maggie collected the skis that had deserted him further up the slope. His helmet was, fortunately, still in place and he removed a quantity of snow that had made his gaiter bulge like a goitre.

Feeling like he had cracked some ribs, Carl did his best to join the other two on a treed ridge, where they watched Justine judder to a stop at the lift station. She appeared to interact curtly with the liftie, and rode the chair back up, alone.

When they got to the station themselves, they realised that the liftie was Roland. They did not like or trust Roland and the feeling was mutual. Hans's assistant worked at Yupik each morning, employed casually, mostly for the rush period and then worked as a relief liftie. He was known to be quietly strange and unpopular – so was generally given the more remote stations. The Ziffers said, 'Hi' out of duty, but Roland's reply was just an over-confident grin, as if he had an amusing dark secret. Roland bunked at Dark Tower and they felt he sided with The Bandits against them.

The snowfields cliché, INXS's 'Falling Down the Mountain', played as they alighted at the top.

'How much money do we have left?' Dolly asked Maggie.

'About four grand each, why?'

'I'm gonna have to rent better skis. I've got to take this seriously. Justine is too good, I fear.'

Dolly desperately needed to win the Interschools and take the accolade with her to Europe.

Down in the valley, the huskie sled ride was returning, following the same track used by cross-country skiers. Many students dismiss the idea of doing cross-country and sleeping out in the snow because it doesn't have the excitement of downhill skiing. But Dolly, Maggie and Jess admire them greatly, often talking about their fascination for it.

On a widened area beside the dog-sled trail, far into The Cauldron, the cross-country students are instructed in building igloos, in which they sleep for a week, making treks on remote trails, generally through the valleys of the back country. Each day, in almost any weather, they venture out, commencing on the sled-dog trail, which their teachers co-ordinate to avoid the two activities clashing on a tight ridge.

Dolly was considering the same next year in Norway, but to do it here was unthinkable. She imagined actually sleeping in The Cauldron, exposed, the fog rolling in, secreting what torments? She had one of her cold shudders and took off, wanting to be on the other side of the mountain. She noted Queen was very popular at stations this season, as she jumped off Gunbarrel Chair to 'We Are The Champions' and headed straight for Heartbeat.

They changed into their walking boots at Yupik and tied their ski gear to the toboggan. Maggie and Dolly shared the task of dragging the load uphill, feeling sorry for Carl, who was still in much pain.

Heavy cloud cover brought darkness early. A few hundred metres up they were out of site of the village and, before a bend revealed the lights of Innsbruck, was the perfect place for an ambush. A tightly packed snowball can be as hard as a rock and an injurious weapon. Carl copped his right below the left eye and went down screaming. The Bandits dropped from the embankment and pelted the other two. Dolly screamed, 'You bastard!' and threw a ski pole that bounced ineffectively.

At the lodge, Carl's misery was obvious and the side of his face looked red and swollen. Carl's ribs were still hurting, and, when asked about his face, responded that he had had a fall. He rejected offers of comfort and went to his room, alone. When your reputation is to be grinning confidently in the face of adversity, moments like this must be hidden.

Maggie warmed herself by the blazing fire, while Dolly ventured out onto the balcony to check the surroundings. A very light snow fell. She did not recognise the musical piece coming from Klaus' room above her. She thought it might be darkly gothic, or imagined it. From the valley, a flute-piece from an ensemble of currawongs, rose in contribution.

That night, Dolly's dream takes her off-piste into the Cauldron, without skis, sliding on the soles of her boots.

It got darker and gloomier as she slipped further into the valley. She saw, through the trees, a space of light where the moonlight had got through, but, turning the last tree she scraped to a stop behind three witches in the clearing, stirring the snow with sticks as if it was a porridge. She felt the slope tilting her to them, and she tried to slide past. The witches screeched at her and tried to hit her with the sticks as she shot past. Beyond the witches, the snow was melting, then became mushy, then icy cold water running into her boots and freezing her feet.

Dolly woke, shivering, and checked to ensure the window was securely closed.

CHAPTER 7

'WELCOME to Chalet Petit!' Klaus announced, as the Ziffers rushed out past the arrivals.

They shouted greetings to Lizzy and Marje as they climbed from the Jinker.

'Hi kids,' Lizzy answered, amused, but her young hosts ran straight past her to interact with the horses.

'Hey! Hurry up out there, then get some firewood,' Klaus ordered. He held the door open for the women and peered beyond the Jinker, concerned at the arrival of their next guest.

While Dolly loved the horses, Harry and Hester, she was equally fascinated by their accoutrements. Maggie and Carl patted Harry's face and ran their hands along flanks, as Dolly examined the leathers and metal link-rings. Dolly gave Hester some attention, concerned about her injury. She then smiled up at *John Thorpe*. Cliff rarely spoke, but allowed fascinated kids around the mountain to hold him up while they engaged with his horses.

But Dolly's contentment was short-lived. Down the road, past Hester's moving head, she saw something! In a quick flick of time she thought there were two people coming up the road towards them; one of them a short man, the other a tall woman all in white – a white fur around her face, the hood with a pointed top, her white edges blurred with the fog, backlit by the glow from a distant lodge. But, as she strained past Carl, Dolly could see only the short man, and, by his gait, it was Hans. Dolly's psyche too often wandered in the no-man's-land 'twixt dream and reality, her *blurred state*, as she called it, where she struggled to distinguish between imaginings and sightings.

Hester jiggled and stomped a foot, causing Dolly to realise that she was pulling on both her tail with one hand and her leather trace with the other. She jumped out of the way as Cliff flicked the reins and uttered an 'E-e-e yup' and jinkered off down the road in what Dolly, not daring to look up, imagined was an annoyed departure.

Hans beamed as he was greeted by the kids and showed no sign that he had quickly discarded a companion. He made his way, carefully, on his short, bowed legs, down the icy steps and in to the warmth of the lodge. There was an audible 'Hmmph' from Klaus, who removed himself, with a glass of schnapps, to pretend busyness in the kitchen but remain in earshot.

Hans warmly greeted the others, who were engaged in lively conversation and the clinking of glasses. He gave Merry a polite, but somewhat wary, nod, and pretended not to see Klaus in the kitchen.

'It's always cosy here,' he said, removing his gloves and sidling up to the fire. Merry, for whom five minutes of socialising was enough, climbed the three stairs to the open kitchen and started stacking the dishwasher. Dolly passed through the lounge and out onto the balcony. Hans watched her move along the handrail, peering out into the fog and through the trees. Behind him, in the kitchen, Klaus heard Merry murmur, 'What's Mary Shelley up to now?'

Dolly turned and, with a pained smile, beckoned Hans to come out and join her. She heard the huskies howling and was shaking slightly when she straightened up from the handrail. Smiling, Hans said, 'It seems the wolves are getting restless. Something bad is afoot, maybe.'

Dolly gave a weak smile, examining Hans' face for a sign of mischief, but the comment appeared to be innocent. Suspiciously, Klaus watched them engage in conversation; both of them occasionally staring off into the distance.

Carl returned to his room, supposedly to do his homework, while Maggie strode through the lounge and out onto the balcony.

'Shouldn't I be involved in this meeting?' she demanded of Dolly.

'It's not a meeting... yet. I'm just flagging the idea,' Dolly responded.

Hans put a hand on Maggie's shoulder. 'It's okay, we talk later. I'm cold. Going in.'

Mark liked to talk to the little Dutchman and hear his stories about history and language. But he was pretty much alone there. While Hans was regarded by many as charming and affable most of the time, many people were sick of hearing his stories of war in Europe. Hans accepted a glass and the armchair closest to the fire.

'Ah, those lockdowns almost killed me. No people, no money. Just like wartime – curfews, rations.'

Jess tried to thwart this diversion; they had just begun to touch on the shooting subject and did not want her husband off the hook so easily. Looking at Marje, Jess pointed to Mark. 'He and Klaus have been out shooting rabbits.'

'Well, they *are* pests,' said Lizzy.

'They don't have to be shot!' said Marje, raising her voice to her partner.

And so it began.

By the time Dolly re-entered the lounge room, adults were all yelling over the top of one another. Hans, who knew a lot about the shooting of people, had no opinion when it came to animals, so kept out of it.

'Quiet!' yelled Dolly, which brought laughter and did actually diffuse the battle. As she climbed the steps to head off to her room, Klaus asked her to get her cousins and go *down* to replenish the wood supply.

'I'll ask them,' Dolly responded.

She stopped in the hallway at the top and wondered if she could, this time, go down into the cellar without fear. She willed herself the courage. But decided it was best she build up to it. She found Carl and Maggie playing games on their laptops, in place of homework.

'Grandpa wants you guys to go down and get some firewood.'

'Are you sure he doesn't want *you* to?' Maggie asked, with the hint of a wry smile.

'No. We are in the middle of gathering information from Hans – for when I'm in Europe.'

'*If* you go to Europe,' said Maggie, 'can you just do the Ziffer deal? Or I will.'

'I've got it all in hand,' said Dolly, 'Can you please go down and get the wood? How about we luge tonight? Can you throw the shovels out while you're there?'

The three of them filed downstairs. Carl and Maggie opened the trapdoor and entered the darkness.

'Dolly! Come here, love. Listen to this!' said Mark.

'You're going to the Netherlands next year,' Hans exclaimed, 'I am very pleased. I must tell you all the places to go.'

'I was telling Hans that I spent time in Freisland, when I studied linguistics. The Freisian influence in early English is significant,' said Mark.

Hans added, 'And I was saying that Freisland was the site of a great resistance movement during the war. But my city of Scheveningen was also a place of great resistance.'

Holding his daughter's arm, Mark added excitedly, 'I explained the shibboleth to you recently. Did you know Hans' town, Scheveningen, was used as a shibboleth during the war to catch German spies?'

'You must go to my town.' Hans looked very proud as he said it.

Mark explained the *shibboleth* to Lizzy, 'If they couldn't pronounce Scheveningen like a Dutchie, they were suspected of being outsiders. Spies.'

Marje attempted to appear fascinated, but, like others, became easily bored by the etymology and history lessons. Dolly's interest drew concern from her mother, who really wanted the European exchange cancelled.

After a while, Klaus leaned over the railing from the kitchen and said to Hans, 'That's it. We've all heard enough of your ridiculous war stories. Get over it.'

Hans replied, 'There is still much in Europe to remind us of the war. A lot of people still affected by it.'

'Hmmph. You weren't even born then,' said Klaus.

'Yes, I'm young. It is you who is over the hill.'

Jess could never quite understand the animosity between these two. She wondered if the *over the hill* comment supported one of the many rumours – that they competed for some woman.

Klaus pushed his chair in the kitchen and made a querulous climb to his room. Merry could invent no more chores so, as Carl and Maggie returned and convinced

Dolly to join them tobogganing, she deigned to rejoin the party.

'They are great kids, all of them,' Marje offered.

'They are wonderful,' said Jess.

She went on to outline their entrepreneurial, athletic, academic abilities. Her voice trailed off, noticeably, stopping short of her concerns about Dolly and her *visitations*.

'They struggled with the lockdowns – like most others.' Merry said the school would have been happy last year to have a break from Carl.

Mark laughed, 'But he's come back with a vengeance. Tell 'em about the school fete, the pet competition.'

'No. I'm still not happy about it.'

'Well, I'll tell 'em, then.' Laughing, Mark raised his arms and spread his fingers to command their attention. 'So, the school wants to attract as many people as possible to their school fete. It's where they make money for sporting equipment and other extras. They want people from other schools – from the whole region. They organise food tents, AND get this, an Unusual Pet Competition to attract young people. First prize is a new skateboard. Carl borrowed the dog from their neighbour, Jeanette. Looks like a dingo/kelpie cross – the dog, not Jeanette. He paints stripes on it and, get this, he passes it off as a Thylacine, a Tasmanian Tiger. He won the competition!'

Hans and Marje thought this hilarious. Lizzy, also laughing, said, 'You're not serious! Surely everyone knew they're extinct.'

'The adults, maybe, but Carl had an elaborate story that had the younger people convinced, or at least curious.'

Merry added, 'And to avoid anyone finding the stripes still wet, he had it in a mesh cage – something a local *blacksmith* might be able to whip up at short notice.' They raised their eyes to the ceiling, through which soft strains of a certain blacksmith's classical music drifted down.

Klaus, at his bedroom window, waved his baton, conducting over the valley and, in the wind, the twisted elbows of snow gums seemed to play accompanied stringed instruments.

Mark went on, 'Contestants had to present a report, on stage, as to why their pet was so unusual. Carl's performance was riveting. He talked about the history of white settlers in Van Diemen's Land, attempting to eradicate the Indigenous people as well as the Tasmanian Tiger. He told how his grandfather – the same one who *might* have built the cage – was hiking in Tasmania, met descendants of Aboriginals who were banished to neighbouring islands and took Thylacines with them. Then, when their people were allowed to return to the main island, they brought tigers back with them and released them into the bush.

'Carl told how these people showed Klaus where to find them and, catching one, he smuggled it back to the mainland on his yacht.'

Merry shook off her disapproval, as a little pride shone through.

'The headmaster said the whole story was brilliant and highly educational. I suspect Carl's sister, and his cousin from across town, had some hand in it. He told the audience that he had to keep it at a distance, in a cage, only throwing sanitized food to it, because human contact would expose diseases and infections for which it was not immune.'

This brought applause from the Innsbruck audience.

'Brilliant!' shouted Marje.

'The headmaster,' Merry added, 'pulled me aside and said they didn't care about the reality of Carl's unusual pet; it was a great effort – educational and creative. I still wonder if it rewards dishonesty, somewhat, if his new skateboard validates fraud.'

But her guests were all still in fits of laughter, including her brother-in-law, who had told the story many times.

'Oh, come on, Merry,' said Mark. 'It's just a bit of shenanigans and there was no stipulation as to *why* the pet had to be the most unusual, even if it *was* due to a paint brush and hair dye.'

More raucous laughter. Merry smiled eventually and lightened up, as she was advised.

'He told everyone it's probably the last one in existence,' she said, getting into the spirit. 'I think his friend, Josh, was helping him with it all,' but she was sure the cage was delivered and retrieved in the back of a blacksmith's ute. While they continued to laugh, Merry added, 'I still think it sends the wrong message.'

'It doesn't end there,' Mark added, still giggling. 'The dog had to be back to the neighbour that night. There's a rumour that the boys and an elderly gentleman were seen out the back of The Anvil washing a dog.'

'In vain,' Merry added. 'Benjamin walks around with faded stripes to this day and Jeanette won't talk. Snubs us.'

At this, Marje and Lizzy were again in fits.

'The headmaster chortles when he talks of Carl. He uses words like larrikin and troublemaker, but always with a bit of a smirk. Says he is inventive and clever, despite all the trouble he has caused over the years. I'm surprised they haven't expelled him by now.'

Hans asked Mark, 'What's that word you have for him?'

'Equaninimiphobic. A fear of calmness, or a fear of there being a lack of excitement.'

Jess was watching her sister, always nervous that she was about to take offence and then the nastiness that would follow.

'Wasn't there a word for that already?' Lizzy asked.

'No. The closest was "Thaasophobia",' Mark answered, 'the fear of boredom. But it's not quite the same.'

At that point, Jess got up and indicated to her sister to follow. They went outside to watch the kids so they could both avoid another boring grammar lesson.

The cousins were scraping the luge track, preparing it for tobogganing. The weak entrance light to the side of the lodge was not enough to illuminate the track, but they had stood glowsticks at each curve so they would know when to lean for the bends. A heavy fog swelled up from the valley and filled all the gaps between trees and lodges. It became denser and swallowed everything beyond the lights of Innsbruck.

As usual, Carl became over-zealous. He leant into curves to go faster and shot over the edge. Steering between trees at high speed, the branches so close, sometimes scraping the sides of the toboggan, he could not put his feet out to stop. The girls were horrified when they saw him disappear over the edge down to Sunset.

They saw Carl sprawled out below, beside the upturned toboggan. The Sunset surface was still icy and very hard. Carl was not wearing his helmet and cried out in pain. Worried for his neck and spine, Dolly sent Maggie for the parents, while she climbed down to help her cousin and ordered him not to move.

It was then that Dolly, looking back up to the lodge, saw the white figure move behind the tree that was just outside the cellar. She had the feeling it had been watching them all along. She trembled and was so absorbed in her own fear, she did not hear Carl's cries, at first. She had her knee on his chest and her hand in his face. She strained to see if the white figure emerged from the foliage.

Eventually, Carl ripped her hand off his face and screamed, 'Get off me!' bringing her back to the problem at hand.

Merry appeared at the ridge, four metres above Sunset and yelled, 'Carl, what have you done? Dolly, why aren't you wearing helmets?'

'Because it wasn't supposed to be dangerous. Carl was reckless. His own fault.'

Jess and Mark arrived and they all scrambled down to help Carl.

'It's alright,' Carl said, getting to his feet. 'I just hurt my back and my shoulder, and my ribs, and my knee. Nothing broken.'

Dolly, in a husky whisper, not wanting to be heard by her vision, either real or apparate, asked her dad if he had seen anyone, or anything strange, when he passed the cellar.

'Oh, for pete's sake, Dolly. At a time like this?' said Merry, rubbing Carl's back.

Jess looked at Merry, once more unhappy about the way her sister spoke to her daughter, but, as usual, it was just at the cusp of offensive, so Jess bit her tongue and avoided conflict.

'We can't climb back up there. We'll have to walk. There's a track that cuts back to the lodge, just up here a bit. Find it before the fog gets thicker. Let's go,' said Mark.

Carl was putting on a brave face, but Merry could tell he was in a lot of pain.

'Are you okay, love,' she said, putting her arm around him in a never-before-witnessed show of affection that served, strangely, to discomfit the others.

As they entered the lodge, Klaus was coming down the stairs. He had had his window open and had heard Carl's wailing.

'Everything okay?'

'Yes. Carl hurt himself, but I think he'll be alright.'

Back in the lounge room they found Hans regaling Lizzy and Marje with stories of snow-filled trench warfare in Europe.

'... and the pitiful screams that could be heard...'

Klaus came from the entrance and announced, 'Ladies, you don't have to listen to that crap any longer. Your transport's here.'

At that moment Maggie ran in yelling, 'The Jinker, you got the Jinker again.'

Dolly went straight out onto the balcony, at the rear of the lodge, squinting into the fog for a shape or a movement. Maggie placed a hand on Carl's shoulder and shook it in a *you'll be okay* gesture. Dolly was seen to shudder as she came back into the warmth.

'How's the training going?' Marje asked her.

'It's okay. I don't think I've lost all my technique during the lockdowns, but I'm not getting the speed or control, I feel.' Looking accusingly at her mother, she added, 'It doesn't help that my skis and gear once belonged to Noah's wife, back when they thought it would snow instead of rain.'

'There's nothing wrong with those skis, or the gear. I bought it all new ten years ago.'

'Fifteen years,' interrupted Mark.

'Instead of contradicting me, you might point out to your daughter the value of money.' Turning to Dolly, Jess added, 'That's perfectly good stuff I've given you. If you want better, you can buy it yourself.'

Then Jess wondered if she sounded as brutal as her sister at times. *Two apples hit the ground, near the tree, one slightly more bruised than the other.*

Hans intervened, 'Now don't you worry about that. I will give you better skis if your parents agree.' He saw no objection in the expressions of Jess and Mark. 'I have some new skis out back. Tuned. I will do special wax.'

'They'll still be pedestrian skis,' Klaus challenged, 'I'll get her top-of-the-range stuff.'

'Well, you must have money,' Hans sneered, 'I see you go to the bank twice this week.'

'You must have been hanging around there to notice,' Klaus replied. He turned to Dolly, 'Besides, you've made me a bit of money this year. Least I can do.'

Moving to the window, Dolly mumbled, 'Thank you. It's kind of both of you,' hoping the subject would change. She was excited by Klaus's offer but held back from accepting it in front of Hans.

Something about the *bank* comment stuck with her and she wondered if it was significant in the unexplained animosity between these two favoured old men in her life.

Then she froze. She saw the white-hooded figure and it saw her, before drifting behind trees.

'Come here,' she gestured to the room, hoping someone would quickly witness what she saw, if the figure re-emerged. But there was a look of cynicism from one adult, and concern from others, before her mum moved to her. Jess could see that a heavy fog shrouded the trees and worried about what was unfolding in her daughter's head.

'What is it?'

'Someone behind the trees over there, a woman I think. White outfit. Hard to be sure in this fog.'

In the reflection of the glass, Dolly imagined that she saw Klaus and her dad exchange quick, uneasy glances. Jess put a careful arm around her daughter. A concerned glance across at her husband.

'Well, I can't see anyone. Besides, it's not against the law to walk around out there.'

Hans grabbed his jacket and left, declaring that he would wait at the Jinker. Lizzy stood and took her partner's hand 'Arise Marjoribanks... your carriage awaits.'

Klaus stomped upstairs to his room. As they all said their goodbyes outside, the angry grandfather threw open his window and Shostakovich's 'Symphony 10, Allegro', rained down upon them. Only Harry and Hester looked up to acknowledge.

Lizzy yelled out to the Ziffers, 'I've got new stuff at Little Envy. Please come in tomorrow and have a look.'

CHAPTER 8

MAGGIE poked at her cereal, worried about her cousin, and tried to appear *un*-worried to the adults at the table. Her brother opposite was, of course, unaware, and wolfing down a plate of sardines and sausage.

Earlier, Dolly had been murmuring in her sleep. But then her tossing and turning woke Maggie. She listened for quite a while, wondering what demons, this time, howled through Dolly's dreamscape. When Dolly started to cry and to perform small screeches, Maggie climbed down, got into bed with her and hugged her for the few hours that it took to calm her down.

Dolly woke with memories of her night-horrors and found herself in Maggie's arms.

'They must have been very serious nightmares,' Maggie said. 'Are you okay now?'

'I'm okay. I don't want to get up today. Please tell Mum I've got cramps.'

On many occasions such as this, Dolly's night-terrors were followed by a period of blurring, dizziness, and lethargy. Maggie tried to discuss what she had witnessed during the night, but Dolly was not co-operating. She thanked her cousin but rolled over to face the wall in a foetal position.

When Maggie informed them that Dolly would be *staying in, not skiing*, Jess gave her husband the familiar, but subtle, look of despair. Merry and Klaus looked over in surprise at the news. It was unheard of for Dolly not to go out in any conditions.

As Jess headed to her daughter's room, she hoped it was not a look of amusement that she detected on Merry's face in the kitchen.

Dolly was gruff with her mother and refused to give any more information than, 'Cramps, haven't slept.'

When Jess returned to the dining table, she attempted cheerfulness.

'Maggie, do you want to come down to the village with me? Mark, why don't you take the Sunset route with Carl?'

Mark had not realised what he was agreeing to. Dropping off the embankment, they shot straight across Sunset, jumped off and over the Growler. They weaved through trees at high speed and hit moguls on two black runs before reaching Cannonball, then catching various lifts up to Heartbeat.

The adventure taxed Mark's quadriceps and his courage. Carl was fast and reckless, despite still being in some pain. Many times, Mark feared serious injury but, at the bottom, he was shaken and exhilarated, wondering if he had become soft and taken it too easy as he aged. This morning, however, catching his breath before the ride up to the village, he felt quite youthful, thanks to his nephew's challenge.

Jess and Maggie took the easy path along the side of the road. Jess had always found her niece rather quiet, and could not remember the last time she interacted one-on-one. She was amused to find that, without Dolly around, Maggie was quite animated and talkative. Unwittingly, they timed their arrival at the door of Yupik as the bell sounded right above their heads and caused them both to cover their ears and laugh at the reverberation through their skulls.

After depositing their packs, they decided not to wait for Mark and Carl, but, instead, headed up Heartbeat and across to Wombat. Unlike Dolly, they were not in training and decided to do as many different runs as they could. Jess was impressed at how the little girl she had once taught to ski, was equal to, or sometimes ahead of her, especially on the most difficult slopes. They challenged each other all morning, with a few falls and many laughs.

Around midday they were heading back to the village to meet Carl and Mark for lunch. On the chair, Maggie chattered away, reminding her aunt of her superiority and reliving some of their more spectacular falls. But then Jess turned to her and asked, 'Have you noticed Dolly, umm, acting strangely lately?'

'No,' Maggie lied. 'Why?'

Jess knew that anything she said would probably get back to Dolly, so she continued cautiously.

'Oh, she might have been badly affected by the lockdowns, as you all were. The isolation, strange new world, restrictions. Does she seem a bit upset at times?'

'No more than usual, you know what I mean, Dolly's a bit different. I love her. She's my best friend.'

Jess shifted the focus.

'I'm going to miss her so much if she goes to Europe next year.'

Maggie agreed that she would be saddened also.

'We do so much together. I don't know how I'll stand it.'

'I don't know how *I* will cope,' Jess added. 'And we will have an empty nest. You and Carl will have to visit more than you do. She might find me knocking on her door in Holland after a month.'

'I'm coming with you. What do you mean *if* she goes?'

'Oh, nothing really, just all the arrangements and worry about further virus restrictions.' Jess was cautious. She was very concerned about Dolly's problems. She was aware that the *cramps* were not due for another week or more.

'Life just won't be the same,' Maggie lamented.

'Well, we tell ourselves that the nine months will go very quickly.'

Besides being her part-time tutor, Jess wondered if Dolly provided much of the big sister, or even *mother-daughter* closeness that the stoical Merry could not, to Maggie.

'I know I shouldn't stand in her way. She wants to be a champion skier and expand her academic horizons.'

'I meant to ask her, how can you ski in the Netherlands? My dad asked me that as if it was all made up.'

Jess smiled and said, 'Tell your dad that the school in Arnhem has a campus in Norway, a place called Stryn. They go for weeks at a time. It's on a glacier with snow all year round.'

Their chair approached the top of Copperhead to the sound of Deadstar's 'Deeper Water'. Maggie giggled.

'It's funny, sometimes Dolly starts singing a different song to the one that's playing, like she hears something that's not there.'

Jess forced a smile and stared off into the distance.

They joined Mark and Carl to eat their sandwiches at the table outside Yupik. Across the square, Merry was serving customers on Froster's deck. She paused and returned their waves. Merry did not like skiing, but was resentful that the others played while she usually worked. Mark was laughing with Carl, she noticed. Mark, whose mother was heard to refer to Jess and Merry as 'those girls from the wrong side of the tracks, on the wrong side of the river'.

When they returned to the lodge at the end of the day, Jess found Dolly under her doona and still grouchy. She got very short answers to questions of sleep, pain, and food consumption, so left her alone. She passed Klaus on the stairs and inquired if he had anything further to offer on her daughter, but he merely shook his head, raised his eyebrows and continued to his room with a plate of food.

To herself, Dolly was unsure if she had slept much. In previous years, the excitement of skiing, larrikinism with her cousins, the total change of scenery and routine, was enough to keep Dolly's nightmares at bay – despite the alpine fogs! But this time it was not working. Maybe her dad was right; the unfortunate timing of studying the European wars aligned with the modern war, and a pandemic. *Empty streets, trucks queued at the border and Engelandvaarders*, she thought, *illegally crossing the Murray.* She should have felt much safer in the Alps, but she would prefer, at night, the biblio-insulation of her own bedroom.

Her mum tried to ply her with paracetamol, but Dolly declined saying the pain was easing. All night and all the next day, however, she trembled, sweated and was scared to close her eyes. There were threats to get a doctor, or to ask Hans to take her to the medical centre on the snowmobile, but Dolly was having none of it, the discussions resulting often in angry confrontation.

She walked back and forth around the lodge; Jess watching all the time. She was unsure how to get her daughter to open up, without a fight. Dolly found her father discussing with Carl his school text, Ray Bradbury's *Farewell Summer*. She found this unsettling at first, then slightly distressing. She hovered in the kitchen, listening. *This is completely unnecessary,* she thought. She had helped Carl with all of his books. She had just spent a month on Dark Emu. He never mentioned this one.

Then her mother and Maggie discussing their day's skiing, with Merry. They then talked about Yupik's bell.

'We assumed it was from a local abandoned school or fire station,' she heard her mum say, 'but, it's actually from a shipwreck and yet it's up here in the snow. It's incongruous.'

Dolly flounced off back to her room.

'It's not incongruous. Ironic, maybe. No, not ironic, just out of place,' she was mumbling to herself, and the blurring dizziness started up again.

She plonked herself on the bed and stared out at pillows of snow, imagining herself in Europe – away from the horrors. Maybe with like-minded new friends.

Klaus's strong, poignant music above dragged her mind back to her room in the lodge, where she realised she had carved great grooves into the cedar window frame with her fingernails. She was most angry with her father; their special literary bond had always been confined, just between them. *Yesterday we had discussed Steven Pinker and Melvyn Bragg*, she mused, *now he's consumed in science fiction or the like, with Carl!* While her back was turned, Carl had *done a Bradbury* and slipped into first place.

Dolly knew she was on thin ice as far as her going to Europe was concerned. Adding to the recent night-terrors witnessed by her parents, and her current breakdown, she felt an agoraphobic element infecting even her own confidence. She was almost inclined to agree with her mother, that burdening a Dutch family, in her present state, was unfair. But she desperately needed her European adventure.

Taking momentary inspiration from Wagner's 'Ride of The Valkyries' that thrummed her room, Dolly was determined, yet again, to conquer all demons and, most importantly, to win back the respect she imagined she had lost.

CHAPTER 9

DOLLY arose, determined to change her mindset and address her own well-being. She slipped past the kitchen and stepped outside into the soft snow. She had bare feet and wore shorts and a t-shirt. It was a freezing morning with a light, icy breeze. A team of currawongs chortled in the trees above, and Charlotte, the Snowwoman, smug in her warm attire, gave her a blank stare. After a few minutes of stomping around, freezing droplets falling on her from the trees, she went inside to rub her feet and encourage circulation.

Trepidation infused as Dolly slid in at the breakfast table. Klaus acted quickly.

'Hey love, those race skis I promised you, do you want to go to Chalet Zermatt and get them with me this morning?'

Dolly then looked bright and clear-eyed.

'Yes. Thanks, Gramps, I would love to.'

'You can see my new sculpture while we're there.'

'Great. I'll be ready in twenty minutes.'

'How are you feeling?' Jess asked, trying not to sound concerned.

When Dolly replied that she was *fine* – in a *fine* voice, there were quick glances shared in the kitchen. Trying to maintain the mood, Jess offered to meet Dolly later in the day, to do some training, to which Dolly responded positively and felt a little ashamed over her petulance from the day before.

When she arrived with her grandfather, at the village square, she was reminded of the animosity between Hans and Klaus, as the latter waited for her at Heartbeat chair, while she stowed her old skis at Yupik. The sometimes jolly and affable Klaus knew just about everyone and greeted many mountain staff with a wave and a loud greeting. On their way up they could see Chalet Zermatt off to the left, and, below that, Dolly was sure it was The Bandits practicing at Half Pipe, a long way off. A taller figure finished his run and stopped to stare up at the lift. She felt it was Barker – but how could he have known to stop and look?

Alighting at the top, Dolly needed to walk the hundred metres down to Chalet Zermatt. She watched her grandfather ski down and realised she had not seen him ski in years. She was still in awe of the *naturalness* of his movement. Despite the turns and bumps along the way down to Zermatt, only Klaus's knees seemed to piston up and down a little – his torso moved along smoothly as if on a conveyor belt. Despite his advanced age, she felt he could probably out-ski anyone on the mountain.

Chalet Zermatt was a boutique hotel with accommodation, fine dining, a few exclusive retail shops and a ski hire. Around the walls of the lobby were bronze statues of ski personalities, all cast by Klaus. Dolly had been here before, in seasons past, but was not so aware of the socio-economic difference when younger – not just the accommodation, but the patrons as well. While she felt out of place, she also felt guilty they had not paid proper homage to her grandfather's achievements. On wide ledges, on two sides of the foyer, were busts of famous skiers, cast by Klaus in bronze. They were a talking point, for which he was famous on the mountain.

He had kept his latest commission under wraps at The Anvil, then secreted it up the mountain. Now he wanted to reveal his greatest creation to Dolly. He asked her to stop in the doorway to one side. Hans stood before the statue and bowed with a flourish, then gestured to Dolly to stand beside him, waving an arm from statue to granddaughter.

'Lydia Lassila, may I present Dolly Montague.'

'Wow, it really looks like her! Gramps, that is your best yet.'

'Well, I'll tell you something, I worked from photos but, all the time I was thinking of you. You look so much like her, same features.'

'Ha! Maybe I do,' Dolly responded, touching Lydia's cheek. 'Yeah, I think I can see what you mean.'

'Well, tell the others. Maybe then they'll come and see it,' Klaus added, with exaggerated hurt.

Dolly squeezed her grandfather's arm.

'I'm very flattered to be welded into such greatness.'

'Let's go and get those skis.'

Dolly was uncomfortable, being unkempt and wearing cheap gear in the palatial Chalet Zermatt. Some women sat on expensive couches at the huge stonework fireplace, sipping coffees. She wondered if they even skied.

In the ski shop, a short, dark-haired, middle-aged man fussing with customers, appeared to be the manager. When Klaus signalled to him, he indicated with an invisible wristwatch and mouthed, 'Fifteen minutes?'

Klaus nodded and offered to buy Dolly a hot chocolate while they waited. Seated in the cafe, he said, 'I'll miss you, ya know. But I am glad you're going to Europe. I think it's the best thing for you.'

When Dolly put her head down, he took it as maybe sadness that she was leaving. He did not realise it was because she had just seen Justine-from-Trinity walk by with two equally well-groomed friends.

They must be staying here, of course, she thought. She then willed the statue in their foyer, to be an *exact* replica of herself.

'But be very careful,' Klaus added. 'If the plague explodes again, I want you home straight away.'

Dolly sensed that Peter, the manager, was not impressed by her old boots, but Klaus had not offered to rent top-of-the-range boots along with the skis. *It didn't matter*, she thought, her boots should not impact the performance of the skis. They were beautiful skis, perfectly waxed and of a refinement she had only seen in magazines. She had never imagined wearing them herself – at least not at this stage of her career.

Standing in the skis, waiting for Klaus to clip into his, she felt instantly faster – before even moving. She followed him carefully down to the chair. Despite her stationary impression, the skis felt strange. They were overly responsive and Dolly worried that she would not learn to use them properly before the Interschools races.

'We're going way out,' Klaus said, indicating far beyond the Summit. 'There's a big, wide area where you won't damage the skis after Sidesaddle, almost off-piste.'

They commuted four runs and four lifts before finally alighting to Dua Lipa's 'Levitating'. All the while, Dolly felt like it was her first time on ice skates. She gingerly followed Klaus to the remote slope where they pulled up beneath a rocky outcrop.

'See that mogul over there? That'll be your first gate. I'll plant my skis at the right intervals for gates two and three.'

'Okay. I hope I can do it. These skis take a bit of getting used to. They're fast and unforgiving.'

'Now I want you to take this in,' Klaus put his hand on her shoulder and gave Dolly his serious look, that said *concentrate or else*. 'I watched you and that girl compete before.'

'Justine?'

'Yes. I didn't interfere when you were younger. I wanted it to be just a fun, learning experience. But now you should take it seriously.' Klaus explained that, while she and Justine clearly out-shone the competition, they both made a fundamental error.

'You try to turn too sharply. While straight lines might be the shortest route, they're not always the quickest. A sharp turn slows you down. Go a little wider, just a little. These skis will respond to the turn, and you'll complete it faster. You'll be off to the next gate quicker than if you had dug in and chattered.'

With each run they had to negotiate a fog-filled valley to take a slope across to Summit chair in order to get back to the top of the practice slope. Dolly struggled on the first few, but when she became accustomed to the dynamics of the new skis, she could feel the value in her grandfather's wisdom; she felt that she was negotiating the gates more smoothly and faster.

'You are doing very well,' Klaus informed her on the lift, 'I'm impressed at how quickly you adapt. That Justine, she's got a good style, fast at times. She flexes and extends well, but if you keep this little wider turn, not too much, just a bit. You know, in life, sometimes you gotta give a little to gain a lot.'

Dolly hoped that Justine-from-Trinity was not getting lessons as well.

After the last run, she waited for Klaus at the bottom. The

fog had moved on, revealing through the trees, a trail on the other side of the valley. It was the Growler. Away from the village, the Growler wound through twenty kilometres of heavily wooded hillside and Dolly had just discovered one of the very few places where it occasionally looped back on itself to be close to the slopes.

Beside the Growler, on a wide, flat area, sheltered by an embankment, she saw the igloos. Klaus *skrawtched* up to her and she pointed, excitedly. 'The igloos. I've never seen them before.'

'Neither have I. Kids actually sleep in those things?'

Once again, Dolly wondered about the experience of sleeping out in the snow, sheltered only by blocks of ice. She wanted to learn about Telemark and Langlauf, but there was little time. She made a mental note of the location, as best she could. She was anxious to tell Maggie and Carl and estimated they could get close to the spot by following Sunset all the way to the other side of the valley.

While thinking about heading to Europe as they approached the chair–always hopeful of coincidence or irony–Dolly hoped Icehouse would be playing 'Great Southern Land', a common anthem at the resort, but she had to settle for Tame Impala.

As the lift launched them upwards, Klaus announced, 'There go those bastards who hurt the horse. If we had proof, I'd take to 'em with a branding iron.'

Dolly saw the Bandits slide off below her, roughly in the direction of the igloos.

'I've gotta go 'n check on Hester again today. I'll see what Taffy has to say,' said Hans.

'Taffy will be there?'

'Yes and the resort manager. They want to decide if she's fit to keep working. All my years as a farrier have taught me a thing or two about horse injuries, especially the legs.'

She noticed the Bandits disappear over a far ridge. They were at the extreme limit of where you would go if you wanted to catch a lift, rather than have to walk out. *But*, she thought, *I'd rather have to walk up and out in snowboard boots than in ski boots.* She was puzzled, however, that they were in such a deserted area. If they weren't boarding at Half Pipe, they could only be up to mischief or crime.

Klaus handed Dolly over to her mother eating lunch at the square.

'She has done very well. She's adapted quickly to the new skis,' he said.

Turning to Dolly, he advised, 'You better keep at it.'

But then Dolly noticed something else drew her grandfather's attention, across the square. *By his expression, it was someone or something he did not like*, Dolly thought. She scanned the area herself, thinking it was probably Hans, but she could make out no one of interest. She was about to enquire, but said nothing. Lizzy walked over, issued greetings and sat with them eating a pie and sauce.

'Look at you two, healthy sandwiches, wholemeal, salad, I suppose.' Holding up her pie, Lizzy added, 'I'll be as fat as a wombat soon. Marje is already.' Lizzy then reminded Dolly that she still had not been in to see the new exhibits.

'Sorry, Lizzy, we'll be in tomorrow, I reckon.' Dolly was aware that Klaus, still beside them, had concentrated his stare beside the transport office. She then saw The Turk disappear behind the building, in the direction of Dark Tower.

CHAPTER 10

THE morning's hard skiing with her grandfather had tested Dolly physically and mentally. But she felt it had an almost cleansing effect. Riding the chair up Heartbeat, she laughed and joked with her mother, living the sisterhood of previous seasons. She felt somewhat elated and that her determination to make changes was bearing fruit.

Jess did not agree with Klaus's choice of slope. She was not going that remote; she insisted on skiing The Slide.

'Doesn't matter if others are skiing on it, you should practise on the exact slope that Interschools will be using,' she told Dolly.

They caught Summit Chairlift to 'We Are The Champions', and Jess exclaimed how happy she was that Queen was back in vogue. Halfway up, they could see across to The Slide.

Jess said, 'Look, there's hardly anyone. It's as good as empty. We're not going to do slalom though. We'll just race, wide turns, get properly used to those skis.'

Dolly knew that filling her day with skiing would have the additional benefit of dragging her mind away from *horrors*. She thought that, maybe, when she collected her cousins later, she might try to relive the old days with a bit of mischief and *scalliwaggery.* Be more like the Bandits.

'Yes. We can practise there. It's open and there's no one around,' said Jess. 'Let's see how your new fast skis go. You will never catch me, though.'

Dolly scoffed at the challenge, 'Ha! I can beat you on slow skis.'

Mother and daughter boasted and laughed together until they raised the safety bar at the top, preparing to slide off the chair. Queen's 'Another One Bites the Dust' was playing at the top. Mother and daughter sang as they raised the bar together.

'Well, that's appropriate,' said Jess. 'You'll bite the dust today if you try to keep up with me.'

'Is that so, Mother?' Sliding from the chair, Dolly said over her shoulder, 'By the way, I requested a Queen song specially for you.'

'Did you, now?'

'Yeah, "Fat Bottom Girls"!'

Jess took off, laughing, trying to hit her daughter's backside with her ski pole. She realised, however, that Dolly had become accustomed to her new skis very quickly and was proving elusive.

They skied slalom turns for half the afternoon. They had skied downhill for years, but Dolly was pleasantly surprised to note just how good her mother was at slalom. Jess demonstrated the very instructions that Klaus had given Dolly.

When they agreed to part ways, Jess would be going off to find Mark, and Dolly was meeting her cousins at Little Envy. Dua Lipa sang 'Break My Heart' as they jumped on the last chair.

Jess put her arm around Dolly and said, 'You're skiing really well. I think you'll perform beautifully.' Dolly warmed to her mother's approval and affection. She was feeling the old bond return–the way it was before her parents had to be careful around her–before she was a fragile ornament. Dolly also felt a degree of guilt. She wanted to tell her mum about Aurora... and other things... but she held off.

Then she saw the Bandits! They had stopped on a rise close to the lift. Barker gave her a menacing grin and pointed her out to his goons. Dolly felt they were stalking her now, and was convinced they intended to do her harm. Some of her new-found confidence suddenly dissolved. Her mother noticed none of this, of course, and went on talking gaily about the good weather and snow conditions.

Dolly recalled her cousins' bravery, bordering on arrogance, in the face of a possible beating from the trio below. Conversely, she herself shook and her heart raced. Dolly knew she was safe while she was with her mother, but that would not always be the case and she sweated more than necessary inside her ski gear.

While she was not as fearless as her cousins, she could not remember being quite so scared in previous seasons. She remembered being threatened and the odd bruise or snowball in the face, but it all seemed fairly innocuous, she recalled. But that was before lockdowns and worsened nightmares. She wondered, was she just naïve and lucky back then? Or was she irrationally fearful now?

High above Chalet Zermatt she saw Justine-from-Trinity ski to its entrance with two friends. They clipped out and went in laughing. After a day of skiing or training. *Not a care in the world*, Dolly thought. As she continued on her way to Lizzy's office.

'Dolly, look at this. Aren't they gorgeous?' said Maggie. There was a large poster of a beautiful light-cream-coloured dog with six white pups.

'Alpine Dingo,' said Lizzy, 'very much endangered. Found

two pups in a location that I will keep secret, but I'm using the drone each day to keep an eye on them and to see if I can find others.'

'They are beautiful. So very cute,' Dolly said then added, 'Do they bark?'

'Very rarely and only for a short burst.'

'Well, that's in their favour,' said Dolly, smiling at Maggie.

Carl had noticed a damaged wooden duck, which he lifted from a shelf behind the counter. It looked very weathered, with faded blue, green and grey paint and multiple wounds, like it had been attacked with an ice pick.

'A decoy,' said Lizzy, in response to the quizzical looks from the Ziffers. 'The duck shooters float it out onto the lake, then they hide in the reeds and use a duck caller to make a quacking sound. Real ducks see one of their kind on the water, hear the sound, think it's safe to fly in, then they get blasted! Killed by shotgun.'

'Death by onomatopoeia,' said Dolly.

'What's that?' Maggie asked.

'When the word for a sound, well, sounds similar. Like *click* or *pop*. In this case *quack*. Onomatopoeia.'

'On a mat I pee, ah, when I miss the toilet bowl,' said Carl, rather proud of himself.

'Oh, trust you,' said Maggie.

Maggie perused a picture of a pygmy possum peering out of a crack in a rock.

'I love the possum. That's my favourite,' she declared.

'Yes, they are gorgeous, but you'll be lucky to see one,' Lizzy replied. 'They are endangered, killed mostly by foxes and cats. Here they live mostly at Bar'bara Shoulder, under rocks, under the snow.'

'Subterranean Subnivean,' Lizzy announced, pointing to the poem on the poster.

Dolly asked, 'I wonder why it's *subnivean*? Why not *subnevean*, with an e?'

Maggie shouted, 'Who the hell cares, Dolly? Animals are being killed, regardless!'

Carl rolled his eyes and Lizzy internally agreed that Dolly could be annoying. Dolly thought to take up the matter of the spelling with her dad when she got back to the lodge. She would also ask why he thinks Bar'bara is contracted with an apostrophe.

No good bringing it up here, she thought.

'I have the answer,' Carl declared, 'get the duck hunters to shoot foxes and cats instead.' He makes a gun with thumb and forefinger, points it at Maggie. 'Blow their brains out.'

Maggie yelled at him, 'Shut up, Carl! Nothing should be killed!'

'If they're wiping out native animals.' Carl took another shot.

'You're just like Klaus,' she screamed.

'What about the poor possums then?' Carl responded, angrily. 'You don't care about them?'

Lizzy intervened, 'Okay, okay. That's enough! No shouting in here! Look, it's a difficult subject, but it's one where you should sit down, maybe with your parents and discuss calmly.'

At the same time, Lizzy acknowledged to herself that she and Marje disagreed on the very same topic. Dolly agreed with Carl and Klaus but knew that her mum was vehemently in the *Maggie and Marje* camp.

Coincidentally, through the window at that very moment, Dolly noticed the Bandits on the low embankment across the track. Barker stared straight at her. They must have followed her to Lizzy's office, Dolly thought. *They are stalking me*. She needed to strategise an escape.

Just then, Jess and Mark skied to a stop beside the Bandits. They waved to Dolly through the window. They seemed in high spirits. Dolly thought she saw her father say something to the Bandits. Oblivious to the tensions of war, he might very well have said, 'Hello, young fellas, nice day.'

Her mum and dad dropped off the embankment sideways, before planting their skis outside and stomping snow off their boots, at the door. A short while later, the Ziffers left Little Envy with a parental escort. Dolly nudged Maggie to indicate the ambush they had just avoided.

Nighttime trauma was, however, a different story. Maggie had heard her crying and appealing for mercy; she had jumped into her cousin's bed, hugging her until the sleep-sobbing subsided.

A girl can be as resolved, newly rational, self-improved and determined as possible, but it can all fall apart during the witching hour. She remembered the *Ghosts* of seasons past, but now it was mostly violent witches.

In the dream, Jess calls to her daughter from beyond the trees down in the Cauldron. Dolly is skiing beautifully, and very fast, with perfect turns–her mum shouting encouragement all the while. But, after a very long time, her mother's voice seems no closer. Dolly pushes on into the darkness, further down into the valley.

It is not Jess, though. The voice has been replicated by an evil, cackling sorceress, to draw her into the woods. The hag is in familiar garb: all white with pointed hat. Dolly screams but the witch lets out a shrieking, gap-toothed laugh. She removes the stick from the pot she was stirring and points it at Dolly, like a rifle. She then turns and points it to two other witches, further on, who, to Dolly's screaming horror, are beating her mother and her cousin. Maggie and Jess are covered in bloodied chip-wounds and imploring her to help them. The witches screech-

laugh and wolves can be heard howling, as Dolly slips over on the blood-coated slope, sliding downwards to a beating of her own.

She woke, gasping, to find herself in Maggie's arms again.

CHAPTER 11

MERRY served the Ziffers hot chocolates at Café Froster while they awaited fresh weather reports. Heavy winds had delayed the opening of the lifts that morning and a storm threatened from the southern valley. While blizzards were expected to ruin the day's skiing, nothing weather-wise was actually predictable in the Alps. At high altitudes clouds, storms, heavy fog, in fact, any type of weather, could roll through the hills and then leave the stark opposite, a half hour later.

It was not uncommon for the Ziffers to start the day with a clear, blue sky and, by mid-morning, find themselves exposed on a lift, frozen and wet, with faces blasted by icy pellets. At lunchtime, they might find a complete reversal and be back in clear sunshine.

Maggie could sense Dolly was uncomfortable with her and preferred to look down at her mug while talking. Probably embarrassed by the previous night.

While Dolly knew that she had her cousin's loyalty and confidentiality, she wondered how far she had slipped in esteem. She had taught them to ski and led them on dangerous escapades. But now she was exposed as whimpering and fragile, in need of coddling in the night.

Dolly left the table and walked through to the small verandah, rarely used, on the north side of the cafe. She had an aversion to the Northern Valley; the runs and trails were narrow and unpredictable. They were not good for slalom training. But, moreover, it gave her the creeps. Across to her right was Dark Tower. Below, she could see the Den–but not a sound from the huskies. Beyond that was the Haunted Shack, from which they could hear a moaning of tortured souls in previous, more impressionable years. It turned out, on enquiry, that the *moaning* was the sound of the pump within, that supplied water to the occasional ice rink and fire services. Nevertheless, it all fitted the creepy image. Then there was the incident the other night: the white-clad woman and The Turk.

She could not remember who told her–probably Hans or Grandpa–but, if a storm came from the north, it generally blew across the valley and, while blitzing the rest of the mountain for a period, it left the north in peace very quickly.

Merry walked up beside her, enduring the high wind that threatened to remove the mugs from the tray she was carrying. She leant slightly into the force of the gale, looking down at the Den.

'Did you hear the wolves last night, howling for blood?' she asked.

'No. I didn't,' Dolly responded curtly, feeling her aunt was trying to spook her. She then turned and marched back to the table to enlist the children of her antagonist–either real or imagined–to prepare to ski Northside.

Out the front of the café, on the sheltered deck, they discussed weather affected options, then headed off to the resort management office, to find if the Northside lifts would be operating. With Heartbeat closed, it appeared most people did not expect any skiing, and probably did not want to, in the conditions.

The village was deserted, save for a few souls who undertook necessary work. Taffy ran from his four-wheel-drive to his office, clutching a laptop bag in one hand and holding his beanie on with the other. Maggie pointed out The Turk, bravely heading into the gale and down to the Den, carrying a crate of food for the huskies.

'Roland's not at Yupik,' Carl observed. 'He's going into the management office. Guess Hans won't be doing much business today.'

'He has to be open, though,' said Dolly. 'We gotta get to the locker. First, let's find out what Roland's up to.'

They jumped off the deck and ran to the admin office, entering just as Roland was turning from the counter to leave. There was always an unspoken animosity between Roland and the Ziffers. He greeted them with a sneer or a grin of menace. They, in turn, attempted a look of sheer disrespect. Despite his employment at Yupik, and Hans's love of the kids, Roland's dislike was obvious. He was often seen sniggering and colluding with the Bandits.

'Morning, Roland.' Dolly attempted a pleasant tone.

As they were blocking the doorway, Roland managed a 'Hmmph.'

'Are you working today?'

'Kokoda,' he mumbled, leaving.

'Yes!' said Dolly triumphantly. She asked the officer at the counter, 'What lifts are open this morning?'

'Only on the north side: Kokoda, Cattleman's and Big V.'

They left and headed for the locker. Yupik was open but, with no customers, Hans was sorting and repairing gear.

'Ay yi yi,' he said, 'if the plague didn't completely ruin me, the weather will finish me off.'

'There's better to choose from in Europe, Hans. Why don't you leave, and come with me next year?' Dolly joked, but Hans answered seriously, 'Oh, no. Too dangerous there. That bloody Russian. First sign of trouble, you come straight home, you hear?'

They smiled at Hans and stomped their feet into their boots. Carrying their skis, they tried to use the buildings of the square for as much protection as possible, until they were fully exposed to the blizzard.

'Down there. Styx run. Past Haunted. Then head across to Big V,' Dolly shouted as she took off down into the dark valley.

Halfway down, however, under tree canopy and cloud that was barrelling in, she *skretched* to a stop and let the others pass her. She recognised it as the valley run of her previous night. There was an instant foreboding. A thick fog confronted her and she watched her cousins descend into the necromania of her dreams.

'Enough is enough!' Dolly shouted at herself loudly. Fortunately there was no one else around. 'This can't go on.' She chewed on her gaiter and pushed down hard on her poles, steeling herself to strength, and continued, determined.

The fog had cleared markedly where she caught the other two. They had slowed due to debris on the slope–leaves, twigs and occasional small branches, littering the snow. Visibility was still poor. Despite Ziffer gaiters tightened over their noses, they dipped their heads to avoid the full force of the blizzard on their faces. Shooting through the trees, each of them copped a number of branches in the face or neck before they arrived at the bottom of Styx.

They skied cautiously along a narrow trail to catch the

Kokoda lift, which would take them up to where they could choose between the three runs. There was no one else around–except for Roland, who looked lonely, cold and bored. Ariana Grande sang 'Break Free' and Dolly asked Roland if he got to choose the songs.

'Admin,' was his sharp reply.

They got onto the chair and, for a moment, Dolly felt a bit sorry for Roland. Alone and remote–no real friends. The chair moved off, and once she'd dropped the safety bar, she and turned to see him grinning and yelling into his mobile phone, *which must have had poor service*, Dolly thought, because he then went for his walkie-talkie.

The Foo Fighters supported their departure from Kokoda and Dolly pointed to where they should stop on Big V. They *shwesshed* in the soft powder coating, to stop on a narrow ridge. Four thin, orange, plastic poles had been placed there by Ski Patrol, warning boarders and skiers not to venture onto the dangerous run, called Funnel Web, where rain and sun had exposed large rocks the week before.

'We'll take these and put 'em back later,' said Dolly. 'No one skis there anyway.'

Carl and Maggie took two poles each and Dolly pointed to their positions zig-zagging down the slope. Dolly had a gentle practice run, not going fast, but concentrating on her style, trying to imbed the process within herself.

Back on Kokoda chair she was a little disconcerted by the smug, half-smile Roland had worn. But she had seen it many times before. *And he is a weirdo*, she thought. Over on Big V she could see Carl and Maggie attempting to mimic her performance. Carl was aggressive and fearless; Maggie ballet-poised. If Dolly could be infused with the qualities of her cousins, add them to whatever it was she herself had, well, she might be a champion, she considered.

Don't get ahead of yourself, she thought. *No dreaming, concentrate on the job at hand.*

After her fifth run, Dolly was surprised to find no one in attendance at the lift. *This is surely not legal*, she thought, *where was Roland?* The chair had not climbed far when she heard a snowmobile and saw it was the ski patrol coming over the ridge, towing the injury stretcher. She wondered if something had happened to Roland. She imagined him seriously injured on the floor, calling frantically on his walkie talkie. *Why didn't I look into the hut there*? she asked herself. But Dolly saw the patrol had bypassed Kokoda and headed straight across to Big V.

A greater fear then gripped her.

She knew something must have happened to Carl or Maggie. Kokoda chair ride was the longest and slowest on the mountain. Whatever happened was not in a visible spot and Dolly willed the lift faster. But all she could do was climb sideways on her seat and scan the visible areas.

She jumped from the end of the ride and ziffed to Big V as fast as she could. By the time she could make out Maggie waving frantically, twenty minutes had elapsed since she had first seen the ski patrol.

'Those bastards! They hurt Carl,' Maggie was shouting.

'Who?'

'Bandits! He was going flat out, started to turn, they came from nowhere. They pushed him off. He hit the mogul and slammed into that tree.'

Maggie had tears in her eyes and Dolly put her arms around her.

'We'll go and see him.' Getting out her phone, Dolly added, 'I'll call Mum and Dad. Is he badly hurt?'

'They said it didn't look like he broke anything, but they took him on the stretcher, straight to the doctor. He was in a lot of pain.'

'Damn! I've got no reception,' said Dolly. 'We can't go down. They might be waiting with Roland. We'll cut across to Gunbarrel. It'll be slow, we have to stay high, no downhill.'

After a slow traverse, with a bit of walking uphill, the girls eventually got to Gunbarrel, where they sat down in the snow for a quick rest.

'I've got two bars,' said Maggie, holding up her phone and immediately called her mum. She told her that Carl had had an accident, but not how it occurred. *Yes, he was hurt*, she informed, *but would most probably be fine*.

The medical centre was not far from Froster and Maggie imagined her mum would get someone to cover for her, while she checked on her son.

They had always kept their war with The Bandits a secret–apart from a few minor incidents witnessed by Hans–but now Dolly worried. If people learned what had happened, Merry might involve Taffy. When Dolly expressed her concerns to Maggie, her cousin spat out angrily, 'So what? I don't care who knows. They should be charged! Carl's badly hurt!'

Dolly realised she might have sounded insensitive and back-pedalled, agreeing with Maggie. It would be a slow process of two more chair rides and three slopes until they could get to the medical centre. Coming down Blue Shoulder, Dolly grabbed Maggie's arm, then skied her towards the fence. She pointed to the group that had alighted at Heartbeat. The Bandits!

Dolly immediately scooped up enough snow to make two tightly packed balls. She handed them to Maggie and made two of her own.

'Go! Go! Go!' she commanded.

Boarders, as a rule, don't take off as quickly as skiers; they have to sit or bend down to clip their free foot onto the board before proceeding. Maggie was nervous at first, after recently witnessing their brutality, but, once she zeroed in for the attack, she became slightly euphoric, aggressive, vengeful. Even hateful.

Barker conveniently looked up as Dolly approached at speed, unwittingly exposing himself to a rock-hard ball that sent him onto his back and possibly broke his nose. Sitting down, Glenn was not so accommodating until Maggie yelled, 'Hey, shit stain,' and he looked up to receive the same facial injury as his leader.

Ziffing down Heartbeat, Dolly realised they had made a great mistake. They would have to stop at the bottom to remove their skis before descending the stone steps to the square. The Bandits, screeching and baying for blood, would easily have time to catch up and hit them hard.

'To Lizzy,' Dolly yelled, making a sharp left turn. She jumped the track, worried that, if she dropped short, she would damage the expensive skis where gravel had only a thin coat of snow.

It was possibly the thrust of adrenalin that propelled them, but both girls made it safely across and almost slammed into the wall of Little Envy. Dolly opened the door to the entry-porch.

'Shit stain? Really? Very classy! You're getting as bad as your brother.'

'Well, now they can call him *Snow Face* or *Nose Ball*,' said Maggie, stacking their skis in the corner where they would not be subject to damage or theft.

Three Bandits, two of them badly hurt, *skerrrawched* to a hostile halt, spraying snow down onto the track. The girls were pleasantly amazed to find Carl sitting there on a bar stool, with his back to the window, enjoying a hot chocolate and marshmallows.

'Carl! I heard you were dead!' Dolly announced.

Carl grimaced, trying to smile. He was obviously in pain.

'How are you?' Maggie asked with concern.

'Really bad pain,' he answered. 'They think it's cracked ribs. Mum's going to call you when the doctor arrives. I have to get an x-ray.'

'Well,' but then Maggie stopped herself from telling Carl what they had just done. It would have given him some vengeful comfort, but Lizzy was sitting within earshot at her computer.

Maggie could see, through the window, that they might have exposed him to even greater suffering. She looked at Dolly, who had also noticed the Bandits across the way.

Well, what did we expect? We created this situation, without thinking and corralled ourselves, Dolly thought. 'How did you get... why are you here?' Dolly asked Carl.

'I picked up injured Duckling along the way,' Lizzy interrupted.

There was a crashing and a rattling from the other office.

'That's Hans, servicing our gear,' she added, coming around the counter to give the girls a hug. 'Was I so interesting that you couldn't wait to come back and see me or are you just collecting the boy? Or,' Lizzy glanced out the window, 'seeking shelter?'

'From the weather, yes!' said Dolly, 'But I was very much affected by the duck decoy story. I was terribly sad. I talked about it all night. Didn't I Maggie?'

Hans appeared from the back room.

'Imagine if the duck realised too late it was a trick, knew it was about to be shot. Just sitting there, waiting. That's what it was like for soldiers in the trenches, or charging machine guns at Gallipoli.'

'That would be terrifying,' said Maggie. 'Better death

comes as a surprise than to be just waiting for that shot ripping through you.'

'Well, that's how it was for many young men in the war.'

Lizzy rolled her eyes and Dolly shuddered. While most people were tired of Hans' war stories, he never failed to prick the sensitivities of Dolly and Maggie.

'Ducks need to be shibboleth-conscious,' said Dolly, receiving a knowing smile from Hans. To the quizzical look from Maggie, she added, 'Know which quacks are fake.'

'And that's enough war for today, Hans. When can you have the gear back?' said Lizzy.

'Tomorrow. You get it tomorrow.'

To the girls, Lizzy offered, 'I will get you two hot chocolates at the taxpayers' expense,' putting a *sshh* finger to her lips.

Hans headed out the back door with Lizzy's skis and canvas bags containing other equipment. Dolly could see him through the rear window, loading his van. Maggie nudged her to indicate that, through the front window, nothing had changed. The Bandits remained on the embankment across the track. Dolly and Barker locked glares. *His was murderous*, she thought. Dolly felt like a heifer at the abattoirs; dye-marked, in line for a bolt to the brain.

They tried to engage Lizzy in wildlife discussions, in order to remain under her protection as long as possible, but she showed faint interest and made it clear that she was busy at her desk.

As Hans came in for another load, Dolly had an idea.

'Hans, these boots are killing me. I've got blisters and a lot of pain. They were Mum's but they just don't fit.'

'Well, come into the shop and I'll fit you for another pair.'

'But I can't ski down in these, Hans. And you've got to drive Carl down... and Maggie's in pain as well. Can't you give us a lift, please?'

'Let me tell you, those young soldiers in the war, in the trenches, had the same boots on for a year. Blisters, sores, full of mud, stuck to their feet, couldn't get 'em off. Trench Foot killed more soldiers–'

'Okay, that's enough,' Lizzy interrupted. 'I've got work to do. Now, why don't you be a sport and give them a lift to the shop? There's a nice fella.'

Dolly asked Maggie to grab the skis.

'Oh, and, Hans, it is really painful to walk, and we think Carl's got concussion and a broken rib. Could you please back the van up to the door?'

Hans was about to complain further, but noticed Lizzy's raised eyebrow, so went grumbling with another armful, then backed the van up. Carl grimaced in pain as he got off the stool to leave.

'You poor darling,' Lizzy said, 'A cracked rib is the most painful thing I ever had. I know just what you're feeling. Every movement is excruciating.'

'We'll look after him,' said Maggie.

'And don't even think about sneezing!' Lizzy added. 'Tell you what, I'll give the girls that shotgun I have. If you are about to sneeze, ask one of them to do the humane thing and kill you first.'

'Will do,' Carl replied, through gritted teeth.

Even with chains on, the van's wheels spun, initially, on the icy Falls Road and the chains rattled somewhat, causing Dolly to worry that their getaway might be noticed by the enemy. Sitting next to Hans, Dolly could see his jaw moving as he told himself silent stories. At Yupik, Dolly rented new boots she did not really need, but felt the cost was worth it. The Ziffers then made their way safely back to Innsbruck.

CHAPTER 12

A RUMPLED blanket of low ground-cloud, like grey/white cotton wool, separated the village and surrounding peaks from the other world. In that special place in the sky, like an oft-lapsing addict, Dolly made another pledge of strength–to be brave and resolute.

The season was getting busier and Hans had hired two more assistants. From far off, at the lockers, Dolly could hear they had European accents, which she wanted to explore. But they were too busy at that stage to interrupt. Roland was there as well and she clomped over to the fitting area, intending to catch his eye. When he looked up, however, it was with mild annoyance that he returned her stare. She was convinced of his involvement in Carl's ambush, but his face gave nothing away.

Despite Dolly's fear of reprisal from the Bandits – and Carl's obvious pain – her cousins walked out into the square, grinning, keen to ski as if nothing had happened. Every peripheral movement made Dolly jump.

Merry yelled out and gestured for them to come to Froster. They complied reluctantly, as they had already lost time. When they got to the deck, Merry put an affectionate arm around Carl and, smiling with unusual warmth, said, 'Where do you think you're going, young man?'

'Skiing, duh.'

'Maybe you forgot that you have an appointment for that x-ray this morning, in half an hour. Auntie Jess is going with you.'

'See you at lunchtime,' Maggie said, attempting to turn and leave with Dolly.

'Wait,' commanded Merry, 'just sit here for a moment.' With customers waiting, Merry sat quickly with the kids at a table for four. 'Now, have you lot been up to any skulduggery? That might be, um, a crime of sorts?'

'No, of course not,' Maggie insisted.

'We've just been skiing. Why?' asked Dolly.

Merry looked at Carl for a hint of guilt.

'Taffy wants a word with you,' Merry said in a low voice, 'Informally. If you have any serious worries about what he asks you, though, you call me, immediately.'

At that moment Senior Constable Jones came out onto the deck.

'Ah! Just the people I wanted to see,' he said, with a touch of the jovial.

Merry offered to get the kids hot chocolates. She then turned to Taffy and offered him *another coffee*, with too much sweetness in her voice for Maggie's liking. Taffy perused the handwritten notes on his clipboard.

'How's your back, Carl?' he asked.

Carl looked quickly at the other two before carefully answering, 'Its fine, thanks.'

'We've got a whole new ski patrol this year,' said Taffy. 'I will have to inform them about Zippies and Bandits and others who routinely break the rules.'

'Ziffers!' said Maggie.

'Let's see,' Taffy mumbled, thumbing through his notes, 'four warning poles *designed to stop people from killing themselves* went missing from Suicide yesterday. They were found on Big V.'

'We weren't on Big V,' said Maggie, far too quickly.

'Roland tells me you were.'

'That's because he hates us. He's friends with the Bandits,' said Carl. 'They were there anyway.'

While Carl immediately realised, *how would I know that if I wasn't there?* the slip-up received a big grin from Taffy. The girls gave Carl a look that said, *I can't believe you are that stupid.*

'Now, the medics tell me they received an injured skier yesterday by the name of Carl Smith, who appears to have gone through the warning poles, taking them with him as he tumbled down Big V and hit a tree.'

'Yes, I remember. That's how it happened. I'm in a lot of pain. Lucky to be alive,' said Carl.

'Roland says he saw you lot practising slalom with those poles?'

Dolly piped up, 'You said it happened on Big V. Roland can't see Big V from his station over at the bottom of Kokoda.'

'Yeah. Ask him why he's lying to police,' said Maggie.

'Well, if the ski patrol could prove that you *had* removed the poles, you would be banned from the mountain,' Taffy warned.

'Maybe Roland's satellite vision tells him which snowboarders injured Hester,' said Dolly.

'Has anything been done about that?' Maggie asked.

Taffy had intended to warn or intimidate the kids, but felt the roles had been reversed somewhat. His aggression was further dissuaded when Hans exited the cafe taking the table next to them. Hans greeted everyone enthusiastically, read his newspaper and waited for his coffee. Merry brought out a tray that contained Hans' steaming keep-cup, as well as the drinks for Taffy and the Ziffers. She also placed a muffin on the table for Taffy, asking him, 'How's your stomach now?'

'Still griping, still in pain,' he answered, grimacing theatrically.

'Well, this is genuinely gluten free. You should be more careful about who feeds you,' she said, rather curtly, then returned inside.

'Are we going to be arrested?' asked Carl mischievously, as if being arrested was just another amusement.

'Maybe,' Taffy answered, sipping his coffee.

'You can't arrest us,' said Maggie. 'I'll go and get my mum and Dolly's parents have to be here. We want to speak to a lawyer.'

Taffy smiled.

'No, no, I'm not arresting you. Not just now, anyway. It's not an interview, we're just having a friendly chat, is all. Nothing to get upset about.' Taffy returned to his notes and continued, 'Now, someone has been snooping around the igloos while the students are out telemarketing, messing with their stuff. One time, throwing snowballs at 'em. A snowboarder said it looked like Ziffers over that way.'

'They *telemark*. They don't *telemarket*,' Dolly corrected.

'Careful not to be too smart with me, young lady. Now, I think you three go off-piste quite a lot. You've been seen in the Cauldron and crossing the Growler many times.'

'It's only to practise where we won't get in the way of others,' said Dolly.

'Well, now that you mention others, two girls were seen on snow cam, at Blue Shoulder chair, throwing snowballs at boarders. Looked a lot like you two. They had very distinctive neck gaiters.'

The girls returned to their stoic expressions and said nothing.

'Now, I've warned you before about throwing snowballs. If you packed 'em tight,' *Tightly*, thought Dolly, 'and they hit a little kid in the face, it could cause serious injury.'

Taffy took a satisfied bite of his muffin and a sip from his coffee.

'Let's go back to the incident with the Eskimos,'

'The what?' Dolly interrupted.

'Eskimos! That's what we call 'em, they sleep in igloos.'

'I believe the correct term would be *Inuit*, then,' said Dolly, 'and I assume you are referring to the cross-country students.'

Her indignation had the effect of causing Taffy to 'hrmmph' and run his finger up and down the page again.

'Well, somebody's doing a good job of scaring them.'

On her way to serve another table, Merry attempted to interrupt the police investigation, realising that most customers were watching or eavesdropping.

'How's the muffin?' she asked Taffy.

'Really good,' he answered, smiling, 'tastes like gluten.'

'Well, it's not! Coeliacs should be more careful about who feeds them,' she said, more tersely than usual, which caused a quizzical look from Dolly.

'You are coeliac?' Hans said, excitedly.

'Yeah,' Taffy answered, a little surprised at Hans's interest, 'and I think I got contaminated last night.'

Hans pulled his chair to their table.

'I must tell you. I have wonderful story. In the war,' he gestures to Merry and customers of his acquaintance, to come closer.

Dolly considered the irony: the longer they sat there under the protection of a police officer, the more chance they had of being found and monitored by enemy fighters.

Hans went on, 'When the Netherlands was under German occupation, most people were hungry. The Swedes were sending bread to help feed the Dutch. The Germans realised and made a blockade to stop the bread getting through. In a town where lots of kids had been sick, you know what?' Hans looked at each quizzical face, pausing for dramatic effect. 'The kids got better! They had coeliac. It had never been discovered before. They actually got better being hungry, with no bread!'

Taffy was very impressed. 'Well, I've had it for ten years. I didn't know that's how it was discovered. Amazing.'

'Yes. What had been suspected, was proved. No wheat, no sickness,' said Hans.

'That *is* an amazing story,' said Dolly, genuinely.

'Maybe I need the Germans to stop Beth coming over,' said Taffy, laughing to himself.

'Beth? What's that?' Hans's mood seemed to change dramatically. 'Beth from the bank?'

'Yeah, Beth Wight. I know what people say, but she's been good natured to me. Cooked a couple of meals. I think she stuffed up last night, though.'

Dolly noted the bank reference again, and wondered if Beth might be the issue between the older men.

Hans seemed to grow pensive, and looked over in the direction of his bell. At that moment, Jess arrived to take Carl for his x-ray and, watching his slow progress up out of his chair, they realised he was in much more pain than he had voiced.

With Maggie beside her, Dolly rode Heartbeat chair, intending to get across to Gunbarrel. As they passed Half Pipe, they could see, far below, the seemingly carefree Bandits, practicing manoeuvres. While Maggie swung her feet, smiled and sang, Dolly was very nervous about the outcome of the inevitable battle. She had been thinking about *Gluten- Embargo serendipity*. But she believed their upcoming war would not have a happy ending.

Chapter 13

Dolly leant on the handrail with her mum, marvelling at the morning's sunshine and the beauty of the valley below. The weather that morning allowed them to breakfast on the balcony. There were only thin wisps of cloud beyond the Cauldron. There was no breeze at all and the thick duvet of snow kept everything quiet, except for distant birdsong.

Mark tended bacon and eggs on the barbeque, while Carl, as usual, made his own concoction. He would gather whatever leftovers he could find from the adults' cheese platter of the previous evening–salami, pickled onions, olives, etc.–and mix it all in with his baked beans on toast. The plague's lockdowns had given his classmates a reprieve from the *Mustard Gas* attack that had seen him ejected on more than one occasion.

'Dolly, how about we go for a training run this afternoon?' Jess asked. 'Meet in the square at lunchtime?'

Merry had already said her goodbyes and left for work. They were surprised, therefore, when she returned to the balcony shortly after.

'There's been a slaughter,' she announced. On leaving the

lodge, she had found that Charlotte had been murdered. One of her arms was jammed into the headless neck and most of her torso had been gouged. Her clothes were scattered; some pieces hanging in trees, the hat destroyed, her scarf and gaiter missing.

'Who would do such a thing?' Mark asked.

'Mindless larrikins in the night, or drunks,' said Jess.

The Ziffers all voiced anger, but stopped short of accusation, as they returned to the balcony in earshot of adults.

'Don't worry, guys, I'll help you rebuild her tonight,' Mark offered.

At that moment, the Bandits *skrawched* to a stop right below them on Sunset. Barker stared up, appearing to assess each person on the balcony in turn. Maggie was buttering toast, her head down and could not be alerted by Dolly's anxious expression. The other two Bandits wore no helmets, but had gaiters pulled up over their noses and kept their masks in place. Dolly hoped they were hiding facial injuries.

'I've seen those boys before. What are they looking at? Wonder why they stopped there?' Jess asked.

'Can't be sure,' answered Dolly.

'Well, you'd better not start down in the valley. Walk to the village with us.'

'Mum, we will be fine, they won't bother us and most boarders use the left side of the valley, then different lifts.'

'Well, you be very careful to avoid them. If it's those Bandits, I hear they've been stealing beanies, right off people's heads and they nearly choked one girl, trying to take her scarf.'

Dolly was amused at her mother's *mountain innocence* and thought, *they've done a lot worse than that. We all have!*

The Yupik bell signalled the end of breakfast and the Ziffers clipped into skis on the lip above Sunset. They had given the enemy enough time to be through the valley and

Dolly warned her cousins, 'They'll be very hostile today. Watch out.'

'Sonenunter Gang!' Klaus yelled from his window. 'Careful, stay out of trouble.' Pointing to his ear, he added, 'I hear things!' Then he laughed and waved them off.

They arrived at Yupik, intending to throw their backpacks into the locker and catch Heartbeat as quickly as possible. Roland looked up and gave them a provocative grin. As they passed the counter, he then offered, 'Hans is busy,' raising his gaze to the flat above and then returned his grin to them as if satisfied with himself.

'He's more creepy than ever,' Dolly whispered to the others. 'Let's get out of here.'

They stowed their packs and, as they turned, Dolly froze. The Bandits had them penned in once again. Other groups on the mountain in recent years had eventually bowed to the dominance of the Bandits, either because of reputation, witnessed lawlessness or physical intimidation. The Bandits had established a 'Born to Rule' status, eventually accepted by all–except the Ziffers.

Dolly knew it had to come to a clash. She had wondered in advance if she would crumble, or be influenced by the bravery of her cousins. She was about to find out.

Barker slammed his fist into a locker. The crash must have been heard throughout the building and the force dented the locker door. Roland told the casual staff to go back to their work.

'Never mind. I'll sort it.' He moved a little towards the fracas, but did nothing.

Barker and Glenn wore their gaiters over their noses–gaiters bearing the distinctive Ziffer logo. Carl pushed in front of the girls and, pointing at Barker's, said, 'Did you take that from a defenceless snow woman?'

'Might have,' Glenn replied. 'What are you going to do about it?'

'You three are pathetic,' said Barker, 'naming your little gang after trendy snowboard gear. Ziffers, ha! Very uncool, even for you.'

But he did not get the reaction he wanted. Dolly, Maggie and Carl smiled at one another and then back at him, as if the balance of power had suddenly shifted. No weapons or reinforcements had magically appeared, but suddenly Barker felt his menace strangely diminished.

Dolly smiled at him.

'But they are *very affordable*,' she said, in a sing-song, jingle voice.

Her cousins grinned. In fact, they were grinning so profoundly that they risked bursting into laughter. The Bandits were angrier yet could not do much in such proximity to witnesses and surveillance. They had come to warn and frighten.

'We'll get you today,' said Glenn. 'Youse're goin' down.'

While Dolly thought, *Please don't say youse*, Maggie said, 'Of course we're going *down*. We rarely ski *up*, clown.'

Glenn pushed Maggie off balance against the locker, his anger possibly exacerbated by a painful, hidden bruise. As she made to lunge back at him, Dolly inserted herself between her cousins and the Bandits in that narrow space. She realised instantly that she felt somewhat emboldened. She had noted also, the irony of each time she faced the proximity of real violence from her enemies, the less fear she experienced. *The Fromorians that arose from the depths of the Cauldron and inhabited some of her nightmares, became mere mortals*, she thought.

Barker yelled, 'Oh, what's that stink?'

Carl grinned.

'Carl! You're disgusting!' Dolly shouted.

Maggie just said, 'Oh, Carl,' as she pushed her way out.

The Bandits scampered from Yupik, squeezing their gaiters to their noses. In the square, Barker exclaimed, 'Oh, that was rank! What do they feed that kid, rats and old road-kill?'

'Yes, with some garbage bin trimmings,' Dolly responded.

He pulled down his gaiter, turned to Dolly, and grinned. He had a large red and purple lump under his right eye. Dolly winced and wanted to say *sorry* on impulse, but told herself he deserved it. Up close, she could see he was what her nana would call, *A Good-looking Young Man*, with unusual light blue eyes. There was a silence while they both seemed to take each other in. For years the two groups had challenged each other, mostly from a distance. There were threats and sabre-rattling, but this season there were lockers punched and physical injury. Yet here they were, when the most brutal battle, the serious fighting, was about to erupt, the two leaders were appraising each other with calm interest.

Dolly wondered if the rumours were true; that Barker had no parents and had had to raise himself, often on the streets. *Was this the reason for his aggression?* she mused. Anger at the world, or jealous of those with a home and parents? Dolly had thought about him more than she cared to admit. And he was taking in her features with a softened demeanour. Almost a smile.

'Where did you get the Ziffer?' she asked.

Barker's face showed that he thought it a strange question.

'Same place as anyone else, I s'pose, from the surf shop, why? Glenn got his online, I think.'

The morning's brilliant weather had turned sour; dark clouds shrouded the village and a light rain was falling. The other two Bandits watched from the fire pit, visibly unimpressed with what looked like fraternising by their leader, a fear that peace would break out. Under the eave of Yupik, Maggie stood with her arms folded and a look of disgust.

Barker noticed his unappreciative audience and appeared instantly uncomfortable, that his friendly manner, on impulse, was a mistake. But he was strangely uncomfortable and inexplicably curious.

Dolly yelled to Maggie, 'Let's get out of the rain,' and boldly beckoned them all to follow her to Froster. 'Come on,' she said to Barker, turned and headed for the deck, hoping they, or at least *he*, would follow.

She was gratified then, to find that he had followed her in. The other two Bandits followed slowly, at a distance, but sat under cover on the deck, not wanting to consort at all. Maggie remained scowling over at Yupik. They had entered the café before many others had a chance to flee the rapid change in weather. It had started to pour heavily when they got a table close to the heater, with a view over the north valley. Dolly introduced Aunt Merry and ordered two hot drinks.

'Look, I've gotta tell you something and I don't tell you this to be a smart aleck. Just, I think you should know," she hesitated, wondering if she should have kept quiet. She got enough snide comments from classmates, but she had started, 'When you buy a Ziffer, the money goes to Dollymite Pty Ltd. That's my company. I own Ziffers, well Maggie, Carl and I do.'

Instead of a powerless resentment, or an uncomfortable silence, Barker responded immediately.

'Are you for real? You don't. Serious?'

'I do. We do. I can call Aunt Merry over to verify if you'd like.'

'Wow. That's amazing. How did you–?'

He sounded genuinely impressed, and mildly excited. He was more civilized than she had given him credit for.

'I adopted the word "ziff",' she continued, 'I decided it's the sound you make skiing straight and fast on powder snow. I decided a Ziffer is one who ziffs.'

Merry delivered the two mugs, asking 'Where are the other two?' and was introduced to Barker.

Over at Yupik, Carl had seen the weather and was changing into his walking boots when Hans had come down into the shop, looking around, concerned.

'What happened? I heard loud bang, some shouting.'

'Ah, Hans, farting is such sweet sorrow.'

Maggie came in and said to Carl, 'You are a disgusting little pig. At least you diffused a scary situation, though.'

'You're welcome.'

'Have you seen what she's doing? This is bloody ridiculous. We better go over there and check, before she asks him to marry her!'

Carl and Maggie strode confidently past the two on the deck, refusing to be intimidated and took up a table near the barista, away from Dolly. Their mum came with two mugs of hot chocolate.

'No good for skiing,' she said, indicating the pelting at the window. 'Who's that with Dolly?'

'That's one of the scumbags who murdered Charlotte, we think,' said Maggie.

'The other two are on the deck,' said Carl, pointing them out. 'If they order drinks, let me pee in them before you take them out.'

'Don't be revolting, Carl,' his mother snapped.

'You don't know the half of it,' said Maggie.

Dolly indicated the bruise on Barker's face. 'Did I do that?'

'Yes, you did,' he answered, with fake solemnity.

'Well, I sort of want to say sorry.'

Barker laughed. 'No, you don't, and I wouldn't either. I would have done the same.'

Maggie and Carl stewed over their brews while Dolly explained the Ziffer gaiter business to their enemy.

'... and they're pandemic safe. Ironically, the factory only had small contracts left and was about to close, due to the virus. We've given them enough extra to keep one worker on.'

'Wow, you must be making a fortune.'

'No. We don't make a lot and it's split three ways. I'm going on a student exchange to Europe next year. The only way I got Mum and Dad to pay for it was to offer to put in $5,000 myself, for expenses.'

'Gee, there are many sides to you, aren't there?'

'I don't have all the money yet. Still a way to go.'

Glenn had had enough. He entered and informed Barker, angrily, that they were leaving.

'You two children going to build another snow lady?' he asked Carl and Maggie as he passed.

Realising he had sacrificed much respect, Barker then got up, mumbled, 'See ya,' and left.

Dolly ignored the glares from Maggie and Carl and got up to assess the weather down North Valley. She saw Roland trudging past the Den in the heavy rain, towards Dark Tower. Although he was never known to ski, Roland always carried a single ski pole when he was walking around. He would often wave it about, as if warding off invisible attackers. His liftie duties were probably cancelled for the morning and, as he got closer to Dark Tower, Dolly could see The Turk yelling to Roland from the Den. He turned and pointed his pole at Froster. Dolly felt it was pointed straight at her and gave a little shiver. But he could not possibly see her from there.

She turned from the window to face the disapproval of her cousins. But they were gone.

CHAPTER 14

DOLLY climbed the stairs back to her room, fighting back tears. Her teacher, Ms Rossi, had phoned the lodge to inform Jess that all student exchanges to Europe had been cancelled, 'due to Putin and the Plague'.

Jess relayed the bad news with compassion, but Dolly wondered if her mother was not secretly pleased. Partially numb, Dolly headed up to her room, wanting to lie on her bed and process what this now meant for her. As the anger built in her, she kicked the banister. She wanted to explode. Carl and Maggie were unaware of their cousin's bad news and had been doing some processing of their own. They were angry at Dolly's fraternising with the enemy.

Confronting her in the hall, Maggie yelled, 'You're pathetic! You're sucking up to *him* because you're scared of *them?* Well guess what, we're not!'

'Oh, you have to grow up,' Dolly countered. She balled her fists and the veins stood out on her neck. She tried to push Maggie away to get to her door.

'A grown-up doesn't cry in the night like a baby,' was Maggie's reply, hitting below the belt with the utmost cruelty.

Dolly was fuming. She screeched at her cousin's horribleness and, for the first time ever, hit her! Jess ran to the altercation, where Carl had joined in, grabbing Dolly, in support of his sister.

'Stop it! What are you doing?' Jess yelled. She had never witnessed any fight between Maggie and Dolly before, let alone a physical one, and was shocked.

They would not tell her what was going on, but they knew the truce with Barker was now a serious problem between them. While Dolly was often amazed at the fearlessness of her cousins, she realised it was more than that. They wanted war. They enjoyed it, casualties or not. There were further whispered threats and insults during the evening. Amongst the adults, there was a strange silence. They were unaccustomed to any real problem between the cousins and were slow to process this new dynamic.

In Dolly's room, two levels of seething resentment lay awake for most of the night. Each knew that the other layer was not sleeping, but neither wanted to speak. It was a long night. Dolly *did* sleep for a few hours and, for the first time since she could remember, she had no nightmare! In some of her waking moments she wondered if she was in the wrong, if scalliwaggery and warring with others was fairly innocent. Harmless sorties had always added adventure to their snow trips.

She had often marvelled at the courage or, at best, careless attitude, of the other two, despite real or expected injury. But perhaps it was never as serious as she thought. While she herself was in terror, those fears merely added some colour for her cousins. Perhaps they were right, perhaps she *did* need to toughen up. But then, at other awakenings, she admonished herself for thinking so; it was time to relinquish childhood, to lay down weapons and mature.

There was no treaty the next morning. Carl and Maggie left without saying a word and were gone for the whole day.

Chapter 15

Dolly and her dad were discussing the finer details of her Macbeth essay after an early dinner, while down in the village, hundreds of fairy lights and two large banners announced The Winter Night Festival. It was the highlight of the season for everyone on the mountain. Jess and Merry hurriedly cleaned up and Klaus even helped for once.

Dolly had decided to bury herself in her work and ignore the pain of her most probable loss. She had had spats with her cousins before and they usually blew over, but this time it felt far more serious. However, in her dad's presence, when Carl and Maggie entered the kitchen, Dolly was greatly relieved by the exchange of mumbled acknowledgements before the other two headed for the cellar.

Klaus had sent them to get the sled and prepare it for transporting all their gear to the village. Soon loud clanging and banging arose from under the floor.

'You could go and help them,' Klaus yelled to Dolly from the kitchen. He knew that the sled was secreted beyond the designated *cellar* area, in the far reaches of the under-lodge.

Dolly moved reluctantly, at first, but she had resolved

to show her cousins a braver face and, despite trepidation, climbed down and past the firewood, to the dark alcoves of Tom Farrell's crypt.

'Do you need any help?' she asked. But she was not looking at them; she had taken the torch from behind the bar and shone it around, to every nook and cranny.

The other two had dragged the old wooden sled from back where Klaus had stowed it. In the process, they had knocked down an old box of paint cans, rusted tools and the biggest chainsaw they had ever seen. It looked ancient, corroded and, most probably, inoperable. It had been secured with a chain and Carl was hitting the old padlock with a hammer, trying to open it.

'What do you want the chainsaw for?' asked Dolly. 'I'm sure it doesn't work.'

'We don't. Just want the chain. Got another padlock.'

Dolly was not interested, and their manner indicated that they did not want, or need, her help. She felt there was still animosity. But she also sensed movement in the darkness and Tom's breath on the back of her neck, so she gratefully returned up the ladder.

When the sled was loaded and waiting up at the roadside, Klaus locked up and they all made their way to the village. Along the way, the Jinker passed them with another load of joyous revellers. The village was lit up like a Christmas wonderland and the pub doors were open to favourable weather. Heartbeat was floodlit and snow making machines sprayed their powdered ice through coloured lights.

The fire burned brightly in the square, families toasted marshmallows and music played from the balconies. An enormous snowman, three metres high, had been built in the corner of the square, farthest from the fire. It stood under a large snow gum there, possibly for shelter if the weather turned inclement. Illuminated by floodlights, its coat and scarf appeared to be made from old blankets.

Klaus and Mark went up to the top balcony of Blarney, where they could have a beer and get a view of festivities. Skiers were already curving and shrieking through the technicoloured mist. Carl was anxious to join them but Maggie and Dolly, possibly by tradition, went initially with their mothers to the skating rink.

Hans held a stein of Gluhwein and wore a broad grin.

'Reminds me of Doctor Zhivago,' he said to Merry, '*and* my youth.'

'It's just like *Frozen*,' said Jess. She linked arms with Merry and, rocking from side to side, they sang, 'Let it go, let it go...'

The unusual connection between them did not go unnoticed by Maggie and Dolly, who both smiled. Dolly wondered if their childhood was not dissimilar to hers and Maggie's and if the affection had got sidetracked along the way.

Dolly noticed Justine-from-Trinity, skating with two of her very well-groomed friends, laughing and chatting, without a care in the world, as if the results of the skiing competition were nothing to worry about. *There's consistency for you*, Dolly thought, *always graceful*, *always happy. Nothing changes except that she has a new designer outfit for every day*. Dolly wished her to fall, just once. Or to slam into the railing and scream an obscenity. But Justine was a constant.

Skiing at night was an unusual, but crowded, novelty. After a few runs, Dolly left it to Carl and Maggie; she was not able to practise her turns there and was annoyed that Justine's carefree demeanour still played on her mind. She went to join her parents up on the balcony at Blarney and heard Merry, on the steps ahead, ask Hans to join them. But he had already noticed his nemesis with Mark up there and elected, instead, to drink at the Bavarian, opposite.

From her vantage point, Dolly could take in the full colourful splendour of the night. Occasionally, the scene became psychedelic as a weak fog wandered around between the buildings, over the skating, disappearing and creeping in elsewhere. Like the fog, Dolly noticed Hans leave the pub and move between buildings at times and she noticed Klaus take a surreptitious interest in Hans' wanderings.

In an ill-lit spot beside the Bavarian, Dolly noticed the Bandits push two boys up against the wall. There were raised fists and, she perceived, threats. Dolly thought they might be the two snowboard racers from Baden College she had seen heading there earlier.

'Double, double, toil and trouble,' she murmured.

Maggie and Carl eventually returned to the square and Dolly went across to load her gear onto the sled with them. Passing the Blarney, she could see no sign of combatants or blood. But she felt things moving in the fog beyond.

Carl waved and shouted out to the adults on the balcony. As Dolly approached, he asked, 'Do you think Hans is gay?'

Dolly was taken aback, composed herself, then replied, 'No, but it would be none of your business. Why would you ask that?'

'I heard him ask someone if Klaus has a girlfriend. I see him looking at Klaus a lot.'

'It wouldn't matter if he was. Would it?'

'No, just asking.'

'Well, you're being ridiculous. They are *enemies*,' Dolly emphasised. 'They can't stand each other. Your question is stupid.'

Carl grinned and continued, 'But you know how people sometimes pretend not to like each other 'cos they can't deal with the fact that they're really in love? Like you and Barker.'

Maggie moved quickly aside as Dolly swung her ski pole at Carl's head. It made a loud *thock* as it bounced off his helmet and Carl tried to run as best he could in ski boots to avoid the next blow aimed between his shoulder blades.

It was getting very late and Jess called them all together to head back to the lodge. Klaus could not be found so they decided to head back without him. On her way to join the others, Dolly heard Merry say to Hans, 'I've had too many schnapps and I have to get up early.' She then whispered to him, loud enough that Dolly heard. 'I'd be more worried about The Turk than the German.'

***

As the lights were dimming in the square to signal an end to festivities, the adults agreed to *kick on* back at Innsbruck. Klaus, Lizzy and Merry caught a commuter, while Dolly followed her mum and dad, who were dragging the sled. Halfway up the road, Dolly noticed Carl and Maggie were lagging behind. They had climbed onto a heft of snow, looking back to the village, and were laughing. Dolly turned back and joined them to witness a commotion in front of the medical centre. It was where the Bandits stood their snowboards.

'What have you done?' she asked her cousins.

'Chained their boards to the handrail,' Maggie replied, triumphantly.

'Taffy's there,' Dolly said, pointing to the cop trying to deal with Barker's rage, 'you're going to be in a lot of trouble.'

'I don't think so,' Maggie replied with a smirk, 'You will notice that the banners are covering the two cameras.'

With the lodge in sight, Jess turned and called, 'Come on!

Don't *dilly-Dolly*,' then pushed on, assuming the kids were just dragging their feet.

But Maggie and Carl had other ideas. Sniggering, they asked Dolly to follow them. She jogged across the road in ankle-deep snow, after her cousins. The wind had picked up and snow gums slapped foliage against the sides of lodges to alert the inhabitants of the change in weather.

'Where are you going?' Dolly asked.

'To the stable, to check on Hester.'

The Cauldron was a brooding ocean of blackness at night, with myriad coves and bluffs. On a flat terrace, before you would descend into the abyss, stood the stable. Dolly knew its ominous location and she could see and feel the fog rolling in. She was determined to face her fear. She felt a little guilty, for she had practically forgotten poor Hester and her injuries from the attack by boarders. She knew she had to follow her cousins and tackle her angst.

When they left the illumination of the lodges and dropped down towards a part of the Growler that had looped up from the Cauldron, the stable was revealed only by a dim light from its window. That light became blurred as the encroaching fog consumed it.

Dolly stopped. She knew she could not continue.

'Listen, I don't feel like it. Let me know how she is. I'm heading home.'

Dolly turned her back on the Cauldron and all it contained and soon, guided by the lights from lower lodges, she made her way across to the road. She could feel the wind bringing all sorts of things up behind her. She felt talons lightly scratching the back of her neck. Shuddering, Dolly hurried to the warmth and protection of Innsbruck.

As if expecting her desertion, Carl and Maggie wordlessly pushed on. They ducked under the fence with its warning:

Mountain Staff ONLY. Trespassers PROSECUTED.

The stable doors were padlocked. They felt their way around in darkness, to the window. Carl bent low, bracing himself against the wall while Maggie climbed on his back to peer through the window. It was such an automatic, practiced routine, so no communication was necessary. A wind had started to build and began pushing the fog back down into Hades. It rattled and flapped the very old weatherboards, many of which had long ago relinquished most of the nails that should have secured them.

Maggie could see one horse lying in a stall opposite but could not see the other. The stable was dimly lit with a single dull globe. They made their way around to the rear. A ladder was bolted to the wall, leading up to a small door high up under the gable. The door had a pulley extended over it, where Maggie guessed hay bales would have been hoisted in times past. The ladder looked decrepit and fragile but Carl did not hesitate to start climbing. It creaked and the occasional rung came loose under his weight but, despite her apprehension, Maggie was compelled to follow.

They climbed into the loft, high above the stalls and were immediately aware of the stench of rotting, damp, hay and feed, that almost veiled the smell of horse shit. Positioned behind the few bales that were still intact, and peering over, they could see Harry standing in his stall looking across to Hester lying in hers. The indoor ladder from the loft down to the brick-paved floor was in much better condition than the one outside and they descended quietly.

They greeted Harry with pats to the head and Hester, obviously not sleeping, got to her feet, immediately aware of their presence. Maggie ran her hand down Hester's neck, then her flank, very slowly so as not to alarm her, then her leg. When she held the knee the horse moved in a manner that indicated a little pain, but, when her fetlock was held, Hester flinched noticeably.

'She needs a vet. I'm gonna kill those Bandits.'

At that moment the corral gate hinges squawked.

'Someone's coming,' Carl whispered. 'Quick.'

They moved quietly back to the ladder, clambered to the loft and behind the bales. Maggie heard a rustling behind her. *It must be the wind coming through gaps in the weatherboards*, she thought, as the Alps were no place for snakes or rats, which they had encountered on the one occasion they got Dolly to climb into a barn-loft one night back home. Carl heard it too and had looked around.

'One of Dolly's ghosts?' he whispered with a grin.

The chain on the door jangled as someone opened the padlock. They recognised Cliff's voice cursing as he wrenched open the uncooperative door. He greeted Harry with a stroke of the head and a, 'Hey, boy. How ya doin'?' He then placed his kit bag on a rough-hewn table and continued along to Hester's stall. Caressing her neck, he asked, 'Well, girl. How's that leg?' He made the same examination as Maggie and the horse flinched again.

'That's not good, darlin'. You're in a bit of pain.'

He took a large jar from his bag and gave each horse a handful of the oats, which they seemed to relish. He then sat at a bench beside the table and began to construct a rollie. After placing the tobacco in the paper, he sprinkled in something from a small plastic bag. Once rolled, Cliff seemed to examine the final cigarette approvingly before placing it between his lips and sucking at the flame from his lighter. He leant back against the railing, held the smoke in for a few seconds, then expelled it to the rafters.

The door shuddered open, jangling its chain, as two men entered the stable. The taller of the two sniffed the air.

'Smokin' hooch again, Cliffy! You've been warned about that.'

The other man smacked the joint from between Cliff's fingers and ground it out under his boot, ensuring there was no spark left to ignite the hay.

'Bloody hell,' Cliff yelled as he went to stand but both his assailants pushed him back onto the seat.

'You've been told,' said the shorter man who Maggie and Carl recognised from the resort management office. The taller man, Emil, they knew to own Chalet Zermatt and reputed to be involved in some other developments.

'I can smoke when I'm not driving passengers,' Cliffy answered.

'You'll do what we say,' said Emil.

***

The chattering in Dolly's head never ceased. She was sitting by the fire, reading for her Modern European History essay, but she was aware she was trying to distract from the guilt at not following the other two.

The adults were clinking wine glasses, celebrating their holiday and discussing the festival. Lizzy informed Dolly that she and Marje were to be given celebrity status the following night – they were invited to ride the Jinker with some important people.

'But you don't agree with hooves in the hills,' Mark challenged.

'Well, it's only around the village, not fragile areas and there's a formal dinner afterwards at Chalet Zermatt.'

Mark gave her a look that might have said 'hypocrite', but Merry interrupted, asking, 'Where are Carl and Maggie?'

Dolly needed to think quickly and cover for her absent cousins.

'I think they're outside. I'll check.'

She grabbed glow-sticks from the storage locker at the entrance and planted them so it would appear the toboggan chute was in use if an adult happened to peer across from the lounge room window. The *voice* told her, *well, you might be a coward, but at least you're playing some part.* She returned and informed her aunt.

'They'd better come in soon,' said Merry, 'it's getting very late.'

Dolly grabbed a bottle of red and a bottle of white from the kitchen and asked, 'Who wants a top-up?' Replenishing each adult with their preferred colour, Dolly found the voices continued. She had tasted wine herself and found it repulsive. The voice returned, *You abhor drunkenness, and you criticise people using alcohol to become something other than themselves, yet here you are using it to achieve an end.* Guiltily, Dolly knew how to play them when they had been drinking.

'I have to compare the Russian invasion of Ukraine with Hitler's European campaign,' she began.

A cacophony of slurred voices attacked the issue from various directions, but all issued diatribes against 'that megalomaniac'. She let them get it all out before steering them to the politics of both campaigns. As she walked up and down, Dolly smiled to herself; the adults were unaware of the teacher-student reversal.

'I need parallels for my essay, people, parallels!'

Merry looked out the window and noticed the fog was almost obscuring the glow-sticks.

'Surely they can't be still out there.'

'I'll go and check,' said Dolly.

Mark was criticising NATO, Jess asked Klaus why he thought the Germans continue to buy Russian gas, Lizzy dragged them back to the Hitler comparison. They had been easily manipulated.

Dolly mounted a few steps backwards and raised her arms, joyful of her pulpit position, but needed to stir the pot a little more.

'People! Did you know that as Hitler was preparing for war and genocide, Henry Ford was donating the profits from every Model T Ford sold in Europe to the Nazi Party? Such was his hatred of Jews.'

There was shouting and remonstrating from her students. Klaus stood and declared, 'Not all Germans were Nazis, same as not all Russians support that deranged Putin.'

That should occupy them for a while, Dolly thought, satisfied with her boisterous creation.

When she heard the door opening, she thought, *if that's Hans, we could have a European War right here at Innsbruck.* She was relieved, however, when Carl and Maggie entered. She gave a quick overview of her ruse and asked them to go out and collect the glow-sticks. Carl and Maggie returned, waving the glow-sticks at the adults, they bid them good night and went to Dolly's room.

Laughing, Lizzy arose from her seat, moved to the fireplace and tapped her empty glass.

'Ladies and gentlemen, as educational as this is, I must leave. I've got early work tomorrow.' She alighted the steps to say goodnight to the kids but could hear raised voices in Dolly's room.

Dolly had had to prise information from her cousins. When Maggie had given as much detail as she could be bothered with, Carl accused Dolly, 'Not that you care.' They both displayed annoyance at her.

'You should have been there,' Maggie added, 'but you hate the horses, anyway.'

'That's not true,' Dolly yelled, 'I love the Jinker *and* the horses, if they're confined to the village.'

'Well, we'll deal with it. You're not going to be around anyway.'

'What are you talking about? I've just been talking about that scum, Putin. Europe's not on! He's ruined everything!'

'It's not just about you. What about those poor people in Ukraine?'

Dolly sat on the bed, chastened, while Carl got up and went to the window, peering out into the fog.

'You're going,' he mumbled.

'What?'

'You're going.' His words embedded in the mist he left on the glass. 'We heard Ms Rossi tell Mum earlier.'

Maggie rolled her eyes and lay back on the bed.

'The student exchanges are back on,' Carl added quietly.

The room was silent for many minutes. Carl and Maggie waited for Dolly to erupt loudly, excitedly, eclipsing the important issues of the night. She wanted to, of course, but she resisted the temptation. She internalised, aware of the mood of the others.

Carl attempted to recall all that they had seen and heard during their late-night escapade, without offering any analysis.

'Why are these men so interested in the Jinker and Cliff?' Dolly asked at one point.

Maggie answered. 'There's a syndicate of developers who might be investing millions into new buildings and upgrades. We've all heard the rumours. Well, it sounds like these two guys are in on it. On the take. Getting a commission or kick-back.'

'What's it got to do with Cliffy?'

'That's just a small thing. The head of the syndicate is being shown around and they want him and his wife to have a Jinker ride through the village. Dinner time. Everyone sees them. It's all lit up. Nice public relations.'

'They wanna know who attacked the Jinker and injured Hester,' Carl added. 'They're pretty angry about it.'

'They think it was the anti-development people – the Greenies,' said Maggie.

'No,' said Dolly, 'those people wouldn't hurt an animal.'

'Really? I wouldn't be so sure.'

Dolly was uncertain where Maggie's cynicism was aimed, but it was delivered with bitterness.

'They warned Cliffy. If anything goes wrong or, get this, if he tells anyone about their conversation, or about their involvement, he will *disappear*.'

The other two did not hear the floor squeak at the top of the stairs, but Dolly did and was fairly sure it was Lizzy.

'We should tell Lizzy,' said Dolly, raising her voice a little.

Maggie yelled, 'No! You won't tell Lizzy! Or anyone. They'll wanna know who was at the stable. Management would love an excuse to ban me and Carl from the slopes. You're safe. You didn't break the law! You weren't there!'

'I'm just saying, Lizzy needs to know she and Marje are being used as PR pawns. The Department of Environment used as a visual endorsement,' Dolly said even louder.

'You don't care about them, or Hester, or anyone else,' Maggie responded.

While ensuring Lizzy heard, Dolly knew she was being disloyal to her cousins. But she was concerned they were out of their depth. People disappearing, thugs, big money – who knew what else? Dolly wanted an adult, like Lizzy, to take on the problem. This wasn't some snow slope skirmish between teenagers.

Maggie told Dolly that Emil and a man she thought she remembered as Maurie, the Resorts Management assistant, had some hold over John Thorpe. They were insisting that he drove the Jinker, with Harry and Hester, despite her painful injury, to present Mr Oliver Jacks and his wife to the village.

'They said if Hester was able to pull the cart back to the stables after her accident, then she can pull it again. There's nothing wrong with her, they said.'

Despite their disjointed account of what else was said, Dolly had a pretty good picture. As did Lizzy, outside.

Dolly lay in her bunk that night unable to sleep, turning and rolling, pasting together the whole story in her head. She knew Mr Lawrence, the man in charge of Resorts Management, to be a nice man. *I don't believe he knows anything about this or at least not the threats to John Thorpe or the abuse of Hester*, she thought. But she had little knowledge of his assistant.

There had been stories for some time that certain developers, and corrupt others, were attracting investors to generate construction projects that would make them rich.

CHAPTER 15

DOLLY thought the day would start well; she had had no nightmares, mainly because she had slept little and, when she did, it was coloured by the excitement of her European adventure. She bounded out of bed, appealing to Maggie to do the same. She was unusually cheerful at the breakfast table, despite her lack of sleep. Her parents noticed the change. But, as time wore on, she became more and more annoyed that her cousins had not surfaced.

Dolly also looked up at her mother in the kitchen from time to time, waiting for her to reveal the call from Ms Rossi, but there was nothing. For some reason, although she was bursting with excitement, Dolly did not want to ask; she wanted to be told. She was not sure why. Perhaps she wanted to appear mature. Or she was not sure if Carl should be exposed for eavesdropping.

Carl! What if he's lying?

Dolly looked again at her mother, helping Aunt Merry to prepare breakfast, humming a tune. Like she had no news to tell.

I'll kill him! thought Dolly.

Her cousins eventually dragged themselves to the table, but were still half asleep. Carl was so lethargic he settled for a simple bowl of cereal.

'Come on! I want to get away early this morning,' said Dolly. She went on to explain that they should hit the uncut snow before the hordes arrive. In reality, she was anxious to interrogate Carl. But they were groggy and in no mood.

'You just want to see your boyfriend,' said Carl.

Jess stopped in her tracks with an armful of plates. 'What's this?' she asked, bemused.

'I don't have a boyfriend! I'm not interested in boys,' said Dolly angrily.

'She loves him,' Carl announced. 'Love, love, love.'

Dolly bounded around the table.

'You're an idiot.' She dragged him from his chair, trying to throttle him. Jess dumped the dishes and ran to separate them.

'Stop it, you two!' Jess yelled.

'I'm sick of your rubbish,' Dolly screamed in Carl's grinning face.

'Carl, don't be a nuisance. Dolly, you should know better.'

'Why me?' said Dolly, storming off. 'Tell his mother to straighten him out,' she added, leaving Jess with some aggravation at the comment overheard by Merry.

Dolly got into her gear quickly and skied off down Sunset with aggression. When she stowed her backpack at Yupik, she noticed the Bandits heading to Heartbeat chair. Barker saw her, but ignored her wave and continued on with his mates. She appraised the village snowman but he too looked straight past her with a dismissive expression.

Dolly skied the remote slopes, away from everyone. She had seen the Bandits happily boarding at Half Pipe once as she passed, and on Cannonball, saw Justine-from-Trinity and her friends, appearing to follow each other, relaxed and fluidly ziffing an invisible slalom course.

Dolly was plagued by this seamless and annoyingly constant image of Justine and it seemed, in contrast for Dolly, to highlight her own troubled life. She skied aggressively all morning, without the style she was supposed to be cultivating. At lunchtime she retrieved her sandwiches from the locker and quickly got to her solitary spot beneath Froster. From there she could see across snow-veiled trees, down into the valley and up to distant white peaks that sparkled in the sun and disappeared into cloud beyond.

About fifty metres below her sat the Den, where the huskie team had just arrived. Dolly watched The Turk unshackle the dogs while a thrilled, animated family alighted from the sled. The adventure would have taken them around the Cauldron and back up along the Growler, where they would have seen some beautiful, pristine, backcountry and breathtaking views. The dogs looked a little worn out, but responded, wagging their tails, to the kids' farewells.

Dolly contemplated her world beyond those distant peaks: Kastany, school, Europe, the future.

Why hadn't I asked Mum straight out about the student exchange? Why am I hesitant? Am I, myself, worried about having nightmares in a strange house? Surely they are over.

She thought about Aurora. *It might explain the white witch of my dreams OFF the mountain, but what about up here in the snow? It can't be Aurora. Am I really crazy?*

After stowing the gear and hounds in the Den, The Turk threw a pack over his shoulder. He noticed Dolly, smiled and waved, then started walking to his lodgings at Dark Tower. She saw that he stopped after a short distance and turned and headed up towards the square.

After finishing her sandwich, she put a hand in the snow

and started to push herself up. A black boot stomped beside her fingers and a large body plonked itself down right beside her, almost scaring the stuffing from her parka. Dolly lurched to the side and yelped.

'Sorry to frighten you.' The smiling face of The Turk attempted a reassuring expression. 'Are you okay?'

'Y… um… yes,' Dolly responded. She looked around in discomfort. *This is very creepy*, she thought. If she screamed she was sure there were people near enough to hear her. She waited for his next move, but The Turk just sat in silence for what seemed like minutes.

'They're beautiful, aren't they, the huskies?'

'Yes, they are,' she answered. The dogs had their heads protruding from openings in the Den, snuffing the air and aiming looks up at The Turk, that begged his further attention.

'I've seen you around,' he muttered at last. Dolly gripped the snow and could feel herself trembling.

'Dolly, isn't it?' he said turning. But all creepiness dissipated, as he gave her the kindliest, warmest, smile she could remember from anyone. It felt, somehow, very genuine.

'Yes,' she answered, beginning to smile, herself.

They talked for quite a while about the huskies, Interschools competitions, mountain history and local characters. He turned to her occasionally with the same smile and Dolly noted how this old fellow – well, at least as old as Klaus – had quickly built a comfortable friendship.

'I thought you looked a bit upset,' he said.

Dolly realised she that tears still streaked her face, threatening to turn to icicles as a cold blast came up the valley. The mood returned to a little uncomfortable, while they both sat in silence, gazing out over the Den and the snow-clad trees.

'I remember being your age,' The Turk continued, as he rose to walk off. 'I can only tell you one thing: the adversities of youth become, one day, trivial, even humorous, memories.' And with that, he was off.

Despite The Turk's rather simplistic view, in her opinion, Dolly felt a warmth towards him. She silently admonished those who painted him as a dark character, just because he was a loner, as she was at times.

She lowered her mask over her eyes to hide any redness for her walk across to the lift. She intended to make her way to Gunbarrel, then Suicide.

She skied alone for a couple more hours, then returned to the lodge early, as heavy fog was moving in. She stayed in her room, reading, until dinner time, when she got her food and returned there to eat alone.

After dinner, Maggie came to the room to get her laptop, asking Dolly if she was coming down to the lounge. Dolly responded, petulantly, that she was staying there to read. After a while, she heard a knock on her door; her mum entered quietly.

'Darling, why don't you come downstairs?'

'I'm fine. Reading.'

'Where were you all day?'

'Skiing. Gunbarrel mostly.'

'Well, when you're ready, come down. It's a nice evening.'

She was right. Dolly hadn't noticed, but the wind she had heard must have removed the fog. It was a perfectly clear, still night. The sky had changed as unpredictably as Dolly's moods.

Chapter 16

Carl was awakened by a hand over his mouth. He started to struggle, then heard the familiar 'sshhh' from Dolly, that meant mischief. While he got dressed, Dolly returned to her room to wake Maggie. They crept downstairs without making a sound, in their usual night adventure way.

'What are we doing?' Carl whispered, as he pulled on his snow gear in the drying room.

'Ahh, murder most foul,' replied Dolly.

They followed her out to the cellar door and found that Dolly had loaded the sled with paint cans, rags and the old chain saw. Maggie wondered at the effort needed for her cousin to penetrate the dark under-lodge alone to achieve this, but she said nothing. All three hauled the sled quietly up to the road, careful that nothing fell off. Dolly unveiled her plan along the way and they arrived at the square at 2.00 am.

They needed the curtain of secrecy and, for once, Dolly wanted fog. But that was still below the village, sitting in valleys and moving too slowly. The sky wore a beautiful splash of diamonds and a weak moon peeped through scant cloud off to the side. She was happy, at least, that the banners were still in place, hiding the CCTV.

Taking a rope, Dolly climbed the tree and shifted her backside along a branch, hoping it would take her weight, until she was between the snowman's shoulder blades. She looped the rope over a higher branch, while Carl attached one end to the chainsaw. The old saw was heavy and needed both Carl and Maggie pulling to get it up there. While they held it, Dolly pushed with both feet to get the blade through the upper torso. But it struck something solid and stopped.

'It won't go,' she said, 'throw me up the stick.'

Probing the icy body Dolly realised it had been constructed around a wooden cross. *Makes sense*, she thought, *how else would the arms defy gravity like that?*

'It's had an internal crucifixion! Raise the chainsaw a bit.'

She plunged it through the wide neck, on an angle, and then rested it in the cross-member inside. The timber then worked in their favour, taking the weight of the saw.

Back on the ground, Dolly wrapped a rag around the end of the long stick and dipped it into the red paint. She painted blood on the protruding blade and around the wound. She then asked Carl to find a long, thin twig, while she bloodied the chainsaw's entry wound, behind. Dolly stopped and surveyed the village.

'Look and listen,' she whispered. After pouring some paint into a smaller can, she handed it to Maggie, along with the twig.

'You'll have to get on my shoulders. Carl, you help hold her.'

The eyes were two large balls with pupils. Maggie had been instructed to make a crazed, blood-shot pattern. She had blackened some woodchips with a permanent marker, and gave the massacred snowman broken, black, teeth.

When Maggie was back on the ground, however, they realised she had spilt as much red as she had administered.

'Bloody hell, it's on our clothes,' said Dolly. 'Quick, splash some more on his front and let's get out of here.'

Carl tied everything onto the sled. The fog had begun to arrive and, from the corner of her eye, Dolly thought she saw movement beside Froster. It was brief and she thought, if not imagined, the figure was all in white. But then, she was not sure. She imagined also it was slightly stooped. She squeezed Maggie's arm and, in the dark periphery, thought she saw further blurry movement behind the police station. Then the huskies began to howl.

The cousins donned their ski masks quickly, pulled their Ziffers up and their beanies down. While fearful they had been discovered, Dolly, at the same time, fought the paranoia of being stalked by someone, or something, in white. They pulled the sled in the opposite direction to the lodge, leaving tracks that might not point to them. They took a circuitous route, then got onto the walking track below the village.

They stopped at a corner and removed their snow gear, rubbing it vigorously in the snow to remove the paint.

'We left it too long,' Dolly said, 'it's not coming off.'

She had it on her hands and boots and started to panic that they would be discovered and in huge trouble for wrecking their gear, as well as the vandalism. Dolly got up and stepped to the other side of the track, staring to where the distant mountains would be, through the fog.

'Will all great alpine snow wash this blood clean from my hand? No, this my hand will rather the multitudinous peaks incarnadine, making the white ones red,' she declared.

Getting the *weirdo* look from her brother, Maggie smelt Shakespeare and just rolled her eyes. Carl, who was no stranger to paint folly, said, 'I know what to do. It's oil based.

There's some turps under the lodge. I'll get the paint off, then wash it all in the trough. It'll all dry overnight.'

'That's a lot of work. You'll have to be very quiet but, thanks. Good idea,' said Dolly, turning back to them.

'I'll help him,' said Maggie.

They got back to the cellar and stowed the messy tools of crime as far up under the lodge as possible, without making a sound. Dolly's offer to help was refused, and she detected looks of annoyance, or concern. She climbed the ladder, raised the trapdoor slowly and made her way quietly to bed.

CHAPTER 17

DOLLY could not be sure whether or not they had been witnessed in the square. She could not get to sleep. Maggie eventually crept into the room and climbed the ladder quietly. They lay for hours, each aware of the absence of sleep-sonorous breathing from the other.

In the morning, Dolly hoped that the sortie she arranged the previous night would regain some respect from her cousins. She wanted to return to the scene at first, to see the fruits of their vandalism and the resultant impact on the first arrivals in the square. But she chose caution and encouraged her cousins down Sunset and across to Gunbarrel, avoiding the village the whole day.

Jess was disappointed when Dolly failed to answer her calls inviting her to meet for lunch. After many tries, she left a voicemail, 'I've got some news.'

When Dolly heard the message, she wondered why her mum had taken so long to tell her. She wondered if her parents had been debating whether to tell her at all. Or if they argued about it. She wondered then, about all the items of her parents' debate: nightmares, moods, etcetera, while wandering around the lodge at day's end, trying to act nonchalant.

It was unlike them to be late, Dolly thought.

'Do you know where Mum and Dad are?' she asked Merry, sitting down to eat with her cousins. Klaus answered with a mouth full of food, 'Gone to Zermatt for dinner. They went to look at my sculptures.'

After dinner the Ziffers were heading upstairs when they heard Jess and Mark arrive.

'The sculptures are fabulous,' Jess yelled to Klaus. Then to her daughter, 'Doll, I spoke to Helen Rossi. She got the authority for Ziffer gaiters to be awarded to winners of the heats. The Interschools committee will only pay wholesale but it's a fabulous promotion.'

Dolly was speechless at first. In contrast to her mother's beaming smile, she appeared stunned. When the news sank in, her disappointment was two-fold. One issue was the resentment from her peers, her previous tall-poppy issues, the laughter and snide remarks.

'I wish you had spoken to me about it first,' she responded.

Jess was taken aback by her daughter's reaction.

'Why? Well, I thought you'd be delighted. But, *thanks Mum, don't mention it, Doll*,' said Jess.

Dolly brushed past, making for the door.

'I'm going out,' she said. Of course, her anger was exacerbated by the absence of any mention of Europe.

Jess was stunned a little, then all she could think to yell after her daughter was, 'Well, don't be out late. Don't suppose you want the others along?'

'No!' Dolly snapped.

Jess hesitated in the doorway, wanting to say more, but didn't. She was blindsided by her daughter's reaction. And, as she watched her climb towards the darkened road, she went to the lounge room and spoke softly of her concern to her husband. She then wondered if there was any truth in Carl's 'boyfriend' accusation.

She had apprised her daughter of all the biological aspects of *boy-meets-girl*, but had not adequately covered the *adolescent-emotional*, she thought. They wondered if they should tread carefully, in Dolly's current mood. Mark discussed with her, in academic terms, their daughter's inflorescence, but she wished she had a more engaging sister to discuss the rest with.

Dolly had often marvelled at the relationship between her parents. Sometimes they were chalk and cheese, but most of the time they could be seen laughing together, sometimes in secret, whispering, often affectionate. Overall, they displayed an unbreakable bond. While her dad was a little more inclined towards her European exchange, she wondered if he would still argue in her favour. Or if he had started to shift to his wife's more cautious position.

Dolly had grilled Carl satisfactorily. She could usually tell if he was lying and so she believed that it was good news from Ms Rossi. Debate between her parents must be still raging, she surmised, if they had still not told her.

As Dolly climbed up to the road, she could hear 'Night On Bald Mountain', an angry, aggressive piece, coming from her grandpa's open window. He had played it before, but usually when he was in a bad mood.

A little way along she was surprised to hear the Jinker behind her. Seeing it was empty, she raised her hand, thinking the ride might lift her spirits. Dolly went to Hester and ran her hand down the mare's leg. Horses and driver stared straight ahead, not giving anything away.

'How is she?' she asked, climbing aboard.

'She's okay,' Cliff mumbled, without turning. Dolly

wondered, if the light was better, that she might detect a bruise on his face.

'To the square then, my good man,' she commanded, attempting cheerfulness. The clear, dark maritime sky wore brilliant earth-treading stars over the peaks and the moon was permitted to light the square. Dolly jumped from the carriage and looked up to thank her driver. His face was shadowed by the brim of his dark leather hat. He turned his head a little, but did not look directly at her.

'People told me you call me John Thorpe. Dunno if they laughed. Is it an insult or what?'

'No! No!' Dolly worried, 'John Thorpe is the carriage driver in *Sense and Sensibility.* Jane Austin novel. It's a compliment. A very elegant tale.' *Because you live in literary fantasy land*, Maggie had once yelled at her.

'Doesn't fit me then, does it?' Cliff flicked the reins and Harry and Hester jinkered him away.

In the square, Dolly once again inspected the snowman, who still wore a look of stoical disinterest. Hans had just locked up for the night and came over to her.

'Those bloody Bandit boys! They wrecked him. We all had to help fix him,' said Hans.

'Do you know it was *them?*' Dolly asked.

'Who else? They come to no good, those boys.'

Over Hans's shoulder, Dolly could see the Bandits pass between buildings, heading down to Dark Tower.

Hans was off to the Blarney for a pint, while Dolly went across the square and down behind Froster to observe the boys descending through deep snow.

Why am I angry? she asked herself. But it was a fortifying emotion; she was outside at night, alone, and she felt very little fear. She could see that one of the huskies had its head out of the Den, its teeth bared, but she did not feel the usual trepidation. In fact, the snarl that she at first thought was directed at her, was aimed at Winston. Winston was ambling home across the slope and completely ignored the possible savagery, comfortable in his own aims.

She had promised bravery from herself, to start facing demons, or discount them. *Be more like* Winston! she thought.

She tramped down the slope quickly and yelled to Barker to wait up. He halted at the entrance, facing her with arms folded, while the other Bandits sneered and entered without their leader.

'You've got a nerve,' he said, 'I'm pretty angry about our boards being chained up.'

'Well, I did not do that,' she replied, looking him straight in the eyes.

Barker scrutinised her face under the porch light and saw, he imagined, truthfulness.

'It wasn't the two young guys I saw you beating up, Festival Night, next to the Jagg?'

'That was something else. Do you want to come in?'

'Yes,' she answered, feigning courage. She took a deep breath. She was about to enter the den of iniquity, that worried her elders.

Inside Dark Tower, Dolly found nothing to dispel all the prejudicial gossip, no bright lights or cheerful ambience. It was rather gloomy and cavernous, a tomb of muffled sounds and much blackness. Barker led her along a dark, wood-panelled hallway to the bar, which was equally dim and shadowy. She felt she was the only female in a hovel where scant light barely revealed men hunched, whispering at tables in darker corners.

Smiling, Barker sat on a barstool and indicated for Dolly to do the same. Dolly recognised Leo, the shoveler, at the other end of the bar. The barman had just served him a beer and was consulting him in a low voice.

As her eyes adjusted to the poor light, she did see another female – one who stared back at her, blankly. She wore high black boots, dark grey tights, a black skirt and black t-shirt. Her dark hair was pulled back in a ponytail, revealing the tattoo of a cat on her neck. The other gloomy patrons appeared to Dolly to be plotting or consorting.

She was fearful then and felt that her rebellion had taken her much too far this time; she felt she had truly entered the Underworld. Barker's calm smile was the only safety line.

'Mate! You got a date!' said the barman.

'Just a friend, Dad. This is Dolly. Dolly, Dad, Jack.'

Openly surprised, Dolly responded, 'Hello, pleased to meet you.'

'What do you want to drink?' he asked her without a similar greeting.

'Oh, could I have a glass of half Coke and half Fanta, or similar? Thanks,' she answered, thinking, *I'm underaged and probably could have ordered a double scotch, for all he would care.*

'Half cola, half orange? Riiiight,' he said slowly, shaking his head. 'What about you?' he asked his son.

'Ah, same thanks.'

Leo got up and took his beer to a dingy table, to sit alone. Dolly thought she recognised two other shovelers at the table where the woman in black was no longer sitting. Beside her was a door that read *Smokers Deck*, and Dolly wondered about an apostrophe.

They moved to a small table, not far from the bar. As she sat down, there was a loud creak above her head and Dolly looked up with alarm.

'Floorboards,' said Barker. 'It's an old place.'

At that moment, Roland entered, marched across the room, and left through the *Smokers* door. He returned quickly, looking agitated and sat at a table in the corner, alone, drumming his fingers.

'It certainly is dark in here,' said Dolly, her voice shaking slightly.

'People like it that way. Atmosphere! Anyway, I thought you would've preferred to be with your friends tonight.'

'My cousins? No, I need a break.'

'I meant the other students. I saw busloads arrive today.'

Dolly found comfort in Barker's quiet, empathic demeanour as she laid it all on him. She had no real friends at school; the others treated her as a freak, or a curiosity at best. While she received good marks, the teachers generally ignored her and, at times, she noticed strange looks from them. While the Ziffer gang was fun previously, she was finding it a bit puerile–which she changed to *childish* at Barker's raised eyebrow. She did not tell him of the attempt to revisit her puerility by savaging the snowman.

'I get a lot of snide remarks about my high grades and my strangeness.'

'I don't understand,' said Barker, 'So you're smart and you can ski. From what Steve said, you're a great footballer–and you are attractive.' Barker's body language indicated that, were it not for the darkness, he might be displaying a blush.

'And there have been a few rude remarks, relayed back to me, about my business,' Dolly added, 'You know, my own school has the lowest Ziffer purchases of all the Interschools competitors. What does that tell you?'

'Jealousy,' said Barker.

'Now my parents have negotiated for Ziffers to be awarded as prizes. Can you imagine the reaction, then? I can just hear the sarcastic remarks already.'

'*If* they win one,' Barker said, 'then they would have to

accept it, smiling, knowing you are watching that smile. Stick your chin out. You win.'

He was correct, to a point, she realised. There was a degree of reinforcement for Dolly in Barker's calm strength. They both looked up at Roland as he marched past again and left.

'The stooping weirdo,' Barker called him.

But Dolly reprimanded Barker.

'I know what it's like to be an outsider with no friends to speak of.'

'He's always on the lookout for something,' Barker remarked, 'Dad says he's as miserable as a bandicoot on a burnt ridge.'

Dolly laughed, but then wondered if people saw her similarly; two, mostly, loners. She considered if they were not that unalike. She told Barker she felt disconnected, at times, from her parents, but then, she felt conscious that that was a teenage cliché.

'What's your dad like?' he asked.

'Well, he's a great man. Really, Mum and Dad are both wonderful. Dad has taught me so much and we have lengthy discussions about history and English.'

'So, he's annoying. Like you.'

'Oh, more so,' she answered, 'and he's like my tutor.'

Barker, the person she always saw as a mysterious foe, engaged with her for an hour or more, talking more warmly than any other acquaintance. She occasionally looked across at Leo, attempting to make eye contact, to give a smile, but he seemed content with his beer and his phone screen.

'Look, I want to tell you something.' She looked down at her hands, into the dark corners of the bar, back at Barker. 'Gotta tell someone.'

Barker smiled, intrigued.

'I saw a body. I think it was a body. In the river, back home. During the lockdowns.'

'A body? What did you do about it?'

'That's just the thing.' Dolly hesitated, looked down again, then back. 'I did nothing. Told no one.'

'What? Why?'

'It was really thick fog. I have a problem with fog. But that's another story. No, it's the same story.' Dolly clenched her hands together and looked around again. 'I have nightmares. My parents think I confuse them with reality.'

'Wait on. Tell me about the body.' Barker could see her beginning to ramble.

'I'm sure it was Swaggy. Swaggy Syd, they call him. A drifter. Comes through a few times a year. Camps down by the river.'

'Did you see his face?'

'No. If it was a body, it was face down. I saw the hat, the coat, trouser legs, one boot, all in the right configuration as if there was a body.'

'But you didn't actually see the body?'

'I don't think so. It all happened quickly and... I rode away.'

'It could have been a scarecrow that someone threw in the river,' Barker offered.

'Yeah, but they were Swaggy's clothes. I'm sure of it.'

'Well, if you want my advice, you tell your parents.'

'I have kept someone's death a secret. Possibly a murder.' She looked at Barker's concerned face. 'I think you're right. I probably have nothing to lose. They, like everyone else, already think I'm a bit unhinged. It's not likely I'm going to Europe anyway. I'd better be going,' she said, rising from the table. 'First, where's the Ladies?'

Barker pointed her out of the bar, with directions to turn right, then right again.

Along the hallway she passed a dark timber door, behind which, she could hear the clack of pool balls and Glenn's loud voice. In the corner was a dim light and, rounding it, she ran straight into Cat Lady, who asked, 'What are you doing in this fawsy place?' and kept walking.

At the same corner, upon returning from the toilet, Dolly was confronted by Roland. He grabbed her arm. His sneer was more vicious than ever.

'You don't belong here,' he hissed. 'Get out now and don't come back, or you'll be very sorry.'

'You don't scare me,' she asserted, trying to mask her fear and reclaim her arm. 'I'll tell Hans about this.'

'Yeah? Well, I might just tell him who I saw wrecking the snowman.' He squeezed her arm tighter and said, 'Now, get out!'

Dolly shook loose and, trembling, exited the inn through the first door she found. Shaking and trying to process what had just happened, she realised she was in a complete white-out. Instinctively, she turned back to re-enter Dark Tower, but stopped herself. She was worried about Roland. She made up her mind to face her terror and trod slowly into the mist. Almost sightless, Dolly felt her way to the slope and started to climb. After a little way, she turned to look back at Dark Tower.

There! It's her! The woman in white disappeared instantly, however, behind the building. There was no mistake. In her split-second appearance, Dolly saw the totally white outfit, the hood trimmed with white fur and white face covering. It was sightless.

Her heart racing, Dolly turned away and clambered blindly upwards to where she thought the buildings below the square should be. Holding her arm out for protection, it seemed to take forever. She walked into a tree that shouldn't have been there and tripped numerous times. After falling into a ditch, she started crying. She pulled herself under a low snow gum and berated herself, wanting to be strong.

She had exited Dark Tower in a hurry, disoriented, and had climbed the wrong way. Dolly changed direction, feeling her way through the snow, but encountered more and more trees. Deciding that it must have been the clump between Dark Tower and the carpark, she decided to go down and around. But she failed to clear the trees. She realised that going down was a mistake and she sat, hugging her knees and cried again. Despite her supposed new conviction, she was trembling.

She screamed out, 'Help! Help me! Is anyone there?' The totally silent response further fuelled her terror.

Klaus had told her years ago, when you are lost in the snow, always head *up*. Dolly felt her way out of the trees and climbed. She could eventually detect what should have been lights, all morphed into one very pale glow, suffused by the dense fog.

After what seemed like a very long, frustrating trek, she found a building–not the stilts supporting the rear balcony of Froster, that she wanted, but weatherboards. She felt her way along the wall and up the side, wondering which building it was. She climbed to the front porch, where a dim light revealed the name Jack Frost. Closed for the night, it was a restaurant that she knew below Little Envy. Dolly huddled there for a while, admitting to herself that she was still as terrified of the fog as ever.

Dolly eventually raised the determination to aim herself towards Little Envy. She hoped that from there, she could feel her way across to Heartbeat Run, and make her way down to the square. As she crossed the barely visible track she heard the snowmobile, then saw its headlights intensify.

'Hey! Help!' She stood in the middle of the track waving her arms. The snowmobile stopped.

'Hey! Are you Dolly?'

'Yes! Yes. Can you take me back?'

'Hop on.'

The snow patrolman advised her to hold onto the bar behind her, but Dolly put her arms around him for the ride home. Her forehead hit the back of his helmet whenever they went over a bump but she did not care. She was safe.

'Dolly! Thank God,' Jess exclaimed, wrapping her arms around her when she entered the lodge. Dolly's face was pale, cold and she still twitched a little.

'Darling, where have you been?' her father asked, picking up the wet parka she had dropped and taking it to the drying room.

'I got lost,' Dolly said.

She sat in front of the fire, while everyone made a fuss and Merry made her a hot chocolate. Klaus came down and joined the other adults in firing questions at her.

'Where were you?'

'Why did you go?'

'How did you get lost?'

'Who were you with?'

Dolly gave only vague answers and became increasingly agitated. She finished her drink and Jess said, 'We phoned you, and everywhere else, for the last couple of hours. Then someone named Kelvin called Taffy, saying you'd gone missing. Where were you?'

'Don't worry about it,' she snapped, got up and went to her room.

After a while, there was a light knocking and Maggie and Carl entered. Carl, looking at the floor, rather than at Dolly, said, 'I'm sorry for what I said,' then left.

Maggie put her hand on her cousin's shoulder and asked, 'Are you okay?'

Getting no response, she climbed up to her bed. Dolly was worried she had lost her phone, and turned out the light, lay back and pulled the doona over herself, fully clothed. She looked at the underside of Maggie's bunk where the breathing indicated immediate, innocent sleep. Dolly went over the events of the night in her mind. She asked herself, *Who the hell is Kelvin?* Then, surprisingly, she fell into an easy slumber.

Chapter 18

Maggie sang cheerfully, loudly, and out of tune, as she brushed her hair in the communal bathroom. Jess came in to use the shower and interrupted the performance.

'Morning, Maggs, how did you sleep?'

'Like a baby. I'm ready to hit the slopes. Do you know if Dolly has left yet?'

'She has,' Jess answered, glad the subject had arisen so quickly. 'Do you think she slept well, also?'

'Yes. She was in a good mood and rarin' to go.'

'Did she, ah, say anything about last night?'

'She just said she got lost in the whiteout, disoriented, but she was laughing about it. She wasn't scared.'

'And she slept well?'

'Yes, like a rock.'

Believing Maggie might be quizzed, Dolly had coached her that morning. Not only was Dolly determined to fight her demons, but it was equally important for her parents to witness, or *believe* they have witnessed, her renaissance.

'And, um, that boy?' Jess smiled conspiratorially, 'Carl mentioned–'

'Oh, him.' Dolly had prepared her for this one also. 'Just a stupid guy. Dolly was putting him in his place, she sounded very mature to me.'

Jess examined Maggie's face but probed no further and left the bathroom. Maggie examined her nose in the mirror to see if it had grown.

In the kitchen, Klaus's phone rang. Merry noticed her ex-husband's name on the screen.

'This will be an exaggerated drama,' she said to Klaus's back as he went quickly out onto the balcony to take the call.

At the breakfast table, Carl had a concoction on toast that appeared to be chorizo, baked beans, onion and some dark mush, Jess noted.

'Have you seen Mark?' she asked her sister, who looked to be interpreting Klaus's conversation through the window.

'Said he'll meet you in the square,' Merry answered, distracted.

***

Intending to ski alone, Dolly stowed her pack and exited Yupik quickly, not wanting to bump into Hans, in case Roland had *spilled the beans*.

'Looking for this?'

She swung around to Barker waggling her phone between thumb and fore finger.

'Oh, thank you,' she said, grabbing her property and checking it for damage and messages. 'I forgot it.'

'Forgot to say goodbye, as well,' said Barker. 'Word was you'd gone missing and were overdue at Innsbruck.'

Dolly knew she would have to provide a reason for her sudden departure from Dark Tower and had rehearsed a few responses, but was comfortable with none.

'Umm, I need to talk. Do you wanna get a drink before I go off to practice?'

Highly intrigued by the unfinished business of the dead body, Barker agreed, despite the impatient glares from the other Bandits across the way. As they mounted the deck at Froster, they could see a long queue of customers at the counter. The manager was the only staff in evidence; Merry seemed to be missing. They sat down and Dolly started a little nervously.

'I wasn't sure whether to tell you. I know you can be, well, brutal at times.'

'Just tell me! Now you've got my attention, again!' said Barker, grinning.

Dolly told him about the incident with Roland–why she left quickly through the wrong door. But she quickly added, 'Although he scared me, and I don't really like him, I also feel sorry for him. I wouldn't want any revenge.'

Barker laughed. 'I wouldn't do anything to him. Would've just warned him, maybe. But I won't get the chance.'

'Why is that?' Dolly asked.

'He's gone. Left this morning.'

'Why? How?'

'He was telling one of the shovelers all his conspiracy theories. We knew Roland was an empty-head, but turns out he is a real nut-job. The government was implanting microchips in us with vaccinations, all the whacko stuff.'

'So, Roland wouldn't have been vaxed?' said Dolly.

'No. Dad realised Tyrol had been negligent; he'd somehow got in without vaccination. Someone was going to tell Hans so Roland up and left.'

'Why would he shoot his mouth off now and risk his job?' asked Dolly, 'It doesn't make sense.'

'A lot of people only came 'cos the pandemic created

vacancies up here, while there was a shortage of jobs down below. Dad says those who don't want to be here leave soon as something else comes up. The Turk's gone as well. Wonder if his girlfriend will go.'

'He had a girlfriend?'

Barker laughed. 'He or Roland. Not sure.'

He explained there were stories of a secretive woman, who had been seen creeping up to The Turk's room–but once or twice seen outside with Roland.

'No one's seen her face properly but there's a lot of stories at Tyrol. I don't know what's true. Roland *does* go searching outside a lot for *something*. Like last night.'

Dolly let this sink in. 'Dressed all in white?' she asked.

'Yes, sounds familiar. I think so. Why?'

Dolly told him what she had seen the previous night and on other occasions. They discussed the white-figure sightings for some time. Dolly tried to process it all. She did not mention her suspicions of some involvement with Hans, or maybe her grandfather.

Barker continued, 'Roland is a prime target for anyone running a scam, sect or cult, though. Looking for something to cling to.'

'I wonder if he has parents, or someone, I just can't help feeling sorry...' Dolly was saying, but then noticed Aunt Merry tromping quickly across the square, and her parents and cousins leaving Yupik.

Maggie and Carl went to follow Jess and Mark to the chair but, when they noticed two of the Bandits waiting by a tree, they stopped. They were hoping to catch Dolly on the slopes but now they would have to wait; the resentful looks on the faces of Glenn and Steve, aimed at the deck, gave away the location of Dolly and Barker. Carl looked back at the other two, who had fashioned snowballs and made out they might throw them. Carl just grinned defiantly, challenging them to do so. Maggie noticed Hans on his way across to Froster and pulled Carl's arm so he would follow her.

On the way, Maggie warned Carl to be conciliatory and reminded him of their pact to support Dolly, and, if it meant 'enduring that idiot, Barker, then so be it.'

On the deck Hans looked at Barker with a scowl, then pointed a finger at Dolly.

'Sour! You come and talk,' he said to her, continuing inside. Dolly got up and followed.

'What are you doing with him?' Hans hissed, 'I heard you went to Tyrol.'

'Listen, Hans, I know for a fact he had nothing to do with the snowman, believe me, I know it,' she insisted. Hans loved the Ziffers like they were his own. He examined her face and decided Dolly was telling the truth.

'Okay,' he said. 'Okay, I need a coffee.'

To Carl and Maggie's mild surprise, Barker greeted them.

'Hi, guys. Have a seat.'

Unsure, they were still standing when Dolly returned.

'Dolly, we should get going. They say there's bad weather coming in from the west,' said Maggie.

'Okay, but please sit for just a minute.' Dolly grabbed a handful of Maggie's jacket and gently tugged her to a seated position, whispering, 'Not all my demons are dreamt. It seems there *is* a woman in white.'

Barker interrupted. 'Why did he say, *Sour*?'

Dolly turned back to him. 'My real name is Julia Dolores Montague, after my mum's favourite aunt, Dolores, called "Dolly". I used to love the name when I was little and *was* playing with dolls. Then I started to grow up and hated it. But now I'm used to it. And it's what everyone calls me. It's different.'

'So?' Barker asked.

'Dolores means sorrowful, so I'm *sour.* Maggie is Margaret Dulcie Smith. Dulcie was another aunt. It means sweet, so Hans calls us Sweet and Sour.'

Carl sighed, having heard the story a hundred times. He turned to stare at Glenn and Steve coming towards the deck.

'We're going to Half Pipe,' Glenn yelled to Barker, 'you comin'?'

Barker gave them an ambiguous look and remained seated. Carl was restless also and gestured to Maggie to get going. But they stopped as Hans appeared. He was carrying a steaming mug and sat with two customers at the next table.

'Aah,' he said, taking the first hot sip and burning his lips, 'I been run off my feet. Thank god I got those casuals. Roland's gone.'

Making an effort to converse, Maggie asked, 'So, Barker, is that your surname?'

He laughed. 'No. At school, on your locker they put your first name and the first letter of your surname, like Glenn Sutton–*GlennS*. Steve Lyon – *SteveL.*' He smiled at Dolly before continuing. *A very sweet smile*, she thought.

'My name is Kelvin Peterson; everyone calls me *Kel.* So I got *KelP* on my locker, like kelpie, the dog. So I copped the nickname *Barker.*'

'Oh, not *poodle?*' said Carl. 'Come on guys, let's go.'

'He's right,' said Maggie, 'we should go while we can. The weather is going to turn nasty.'

The two people at Hans' table agreed, got up, and took off to Heartbeat.

'Where did Mum and Dad go?' asked Dolly.

'Over to Gunbarrel.'

'Right. So, knowing Dad's weather-phobia, they'd have headed back once they got to the top, if it looked bad over there and the predictions are usually wrong.' Maggie and Carl stared at her, wondering at her next move.

Hans smiled, seeing the warring tribes at peace and *scrawtched* his chair across to join them.

'It's good to see you are friends now. The Ziffers and the Bandits,' he said, waving his hands in the air and laughing, as if mocking their importance. It reminds me of a wonderful story. You will love this story.' Hans jumped up and told Carl, Rowan and Glenn to sit down. 'You must hear this story. It's marvellous.'

'Another war story, Hans?' Dolly winced.

Hans looked excitedly at the boys, motioning them to sit down. He had a way of creating enthusiasm; getting them to pay attention even if they did not want to.

'Merry! Hot cocoas for all my friends here. I pay.'

Merry laughed and approached to take their orders. 'You're paying, Hans? What, did you win the lottery?'

'Well, this is very important. Today I spend.'

Hans turned back to his young friends. 'I told you about the trenches in World War One, the young men cold and sick, and dying. Not much older than you,' he added, looking at each of the boys. 'On both sides, German and British. It was freezing cold. They were wet most of the time, hungry, up to their shins in mud. Most had *trench-foot*. They were missing their families. They were very scared of being killed at any moment. They saw their friends killed. You can't only imagine how miserable and petrified they were.'

Although people were generally tired of Hans's war stories, he had their attention. They were all imagining the terror.

He continued, 'Well, it was Christmas Eve, 1914. In their trenches, they were missing their families, like I said. Missing Christmas. The Germans started singing Christmas carols and each time they finished one, the Brits would sing one of theirs. And so they alternated. So close they could clearly hear each other. Then, they sang the *same* carol together, and after that, one soldier had the courage to climb out of his trench and put his hands up. I think it was a Brit. They did not shoot him. Instead, a German climbed out and did the same thing. Soon everyone climbed out, a little scared, hesitant at first, but before long, each side could sense that the other was seriously intending to have a peaceful Christmas Eve. They shook hands, laughed together, exchanged gifts. It was truly amazing if you can understand the killing before it – the fear and hatred.'

The kids were spellbound. Then Dolly asked, 'Is that story true, Hans?'

'It is absolutely true. As true as I sit here burning my mouth. You can go and read about it.'

'That's amazing,' said Maggie. 'If only everyone in the world would climb out of their trenches.'

'Yes. Exactly,' said Hans. 'Like you guys have.'

'We just need some Christmas carols,' said Barker, cynically.

'I could fart again,' said Carl, 'musically.'

Hans shot Carl an angry look. 'They were *carols.* You be careful, young man, that could be sacrilegious.'

Carl looked down, pretending to be chastised, then made a mental note to ask Dolly later what *sacrilegious* meant. Dolly thought to check why a word related to *religious*, seemed to have the *i* and the *e* cast wrongly, in her mind.

'So, what happened after that?' she asked Hans.

Coldly, he looked at her, unable to dress up the chilling facts.

'They went back to killing each other.'

There was silence at the table.

'Fair is foul and foul is fair,' Dolly muttered.

***

That night was a bad one for Dolly. At around midnight she had a horrendous nightmare and got no sleep thereafter.

It was trench warfare down the slope she was skiing. Shotguns fired from opposing trenches, down each side of her run. Wooden ducks, with people-faces, were screaming as pieces of bloodied woodchips were blasted from them, sprinkling the snow. Dolly skied halfway down into the darkness of Hades Run, to escape the horror but, rounding a bend, almost slammed into the backs of three white witches, who were stirring the snow with sticks. They turned around and zombie-skeletal faces, grinning, cackled at her through broken teeth. The sticks, when raised, became snowboards, that they tried to slam down on top of her, which Dolly narrowly avoided by pushing off and skiing further down into Hades.

In the meagre light the snow gums gave way to taller, darker, thick-trunked eucalypts. Approaching a clearing, lit by the moon, Dolly found the witch-zombies were already ahead of her and beating Carl mercilessly with their snowboards. They cackled at her again, blood splashing all over Carl's motionless body. Dolly screamed at them to stop and flailed her ski poles at them.

She was screaming for her mum and dad as she woke. Dolly remained shaking and disturbed until daybreak.

Chapter 19

'I'll have a coffee, thanks,' she said to her aunt.

Dolly was sleep-deprived; she was fuzzy-headed and tremulous. She was late getting to the square, although she had taken the shorter roadside trail, completely avoiding the Cauldron. It was so late in fact, Yupik had closed for morning tea and Hans was approaching Froster.

'Since when do you drink coffee?' Merry asked.

'I've tried it before. I'm told it perks you up.'

'Hmm, maybe. Don't believe everything.'

'Sour! Good morning,' said Hans, on his way to the door. 'Another beautiful day, like yesterday. You can't rely on forecasts up here.'

'Morning, Hans.' Hunched over the table, Dolly's hands supported her chin.

Hans was stopped in the doorway by Merry exiting with a tray, adopting a strange smile.

'Ol' pale-face has gone,' Dolly could hear her say, in a lowered voice.

'What do you mean?' Hans asked. 'Who's that?'

'You know,' said Merry, sounding mischievous, 'Beth from the bank.'

'Oh, her.' Hans shrugged. 'I'll have a long black, thanks.'

He then turned and invited himself to sit. Dolly noticed he became somewhat pensive, glancing around the village. After examining him for a while, she said, 'That was an amazing story you told yesterday.'

'Ummm,' he responded, trying to bring his mind back to the table.

'The Christmas truce of 1914,' she prompted.

'Ah, yes, yes, amazing one, that.'

But he seemed to drift off again. Dolly wanted quiet, anyway. She had never been to the bank. They had got Merry to deposit their cash. She knew it was only open part-time and she had heard of Beth, the gruff, business-like teller that nobody warmed to.

She looked up to the top of Heartbeat and imagined her parents skiing beyond, with Maggie and Carl. She pictured Justin-from-Trinity there with her friends, perfecting their technique in preparation for the heats over the next few days. Feeling tired and vague, she turned as Aunt Merry approached. Dolly did not then see the black cloud consume the Summit and march towards the village.

'Long black for you and a cappuccino for you. At least it's got chocolate on top.'

When they finished, Dolly noticed the weather coming in. She pulled her skis from where they were standing in the snow, but was unsure whether to proceed.

'A few people seem to be vacating the mountain,' she said to Hans.

'Hmmph. Hard enough to get staff with the plague 'n all.'

At that moment there was a loud *CRACK*. Hans swung around sharply. Then there was another. The sounds came from the lower buildings behind the pub. Then there was screaming and shouting. Another two loud *CRACKs*.

'That's a gun,' Hans shouted. 'Run!'

He grabbed Dolly by the arm and pulled her as fast as she could run in ski boots. Heading for Yupik, they heard another *CRACK* and more screaming. Yupik was locked. Hans banged on the door, shouting, but the staff had disappeared. While he fumbled in the pockets of his pants and jacket for the key, Dolly turned and saw people running into the square, screaming, panicked and heading for refuge.

Another gunshot sounded as they got inside and Hans threw Dolly to the floor below the window, neglecting to lock the door. The square was quickly deserted and quiet. A lone figure, all in white, with white balaclava, walked into the square carrying a pistol in one hand and a black bag in the other. He pointed the gun into the air and fired another shot.

Hans was right, thought Dolly, *he knew straight away that it was a gunshot.*

'Stay down,' Hans whispered sharply, peering cautiously from the corner of the window. Dolly squatted on the floor with her back to the wall, breathing rapidly.

'He's coming this way! Quick! To the cellar!'

They crouch-scrambled to get behind the counter. Hans lifted the trapdoor and pushed her down the ladder into the darkness. She fell sideways onto his snowmobile. There he *ssshhhed* her again and shoved her into the darkest corner. Dolly was shaking, sweating and panting all at once. This was more terrifying than any nightmare or daytime imagining. It was acutely real. A real gun. A real killer. Approaching.

Dolly had seen Hans businesslike, usually affable, sometimes irritable–but she had never seen him this fearfully serious. She felt she was living one of his war stories.

Then it got worse.

They heard the door slam shut above and heavy footsteps.

When Hans clamped her head in his hands, one of them covering her mouth, Dolly's shaking intensified; her terror exacerbated in the dark by a thin slice of light through the wall that cut through Hans and distorted his face.

Suddenly, a text *ding*ed on Dolly's phone! She should have turned it off! She fumbled in her pocket to silence it. The footsteps stopped!

But then he moved again, and they heard them off to the side. There was audible zipping, clunking and shuffling. Then the side door opened and closed.

Hans felt around quietly amongst his tools. He held up a very large spanner and faced the rear door. Readying for a violent intrusion. Dolly's terror intensified.

Her relief was palpable, however, when they heard the snowmobile from the medical centre next door start up and take off. Hans opened the door slowly and they saw the vehicle, with rescue sled still coupled, disappearing across the slope and through the trees. A lone, stooped figure in the driver's seat.

'I think he'll head for the car park,' said Hans.

'He won't come back, will he?'

'I don't think so, but I don't really know what's going on.'

As they retreated back into the cellar, a strong wind slammed the door shut; the blizzard raced in from the south, worrying all of Yupik's loose weather boards. They could hear the snow gums being thrashed fiercely, foliage and ice hitting the walls. Dolly took out her phone and saw that the text was from her dad. It read: *Blizzard! Calamity here. Racing back.*

From up in the shop, they looked out to the square. People were slowly emerging; most appeared to be dazed and all very cautious. Gloved hands shielded faces from the weather and other dangers.

The usually cheerful vacation atmosphere had left the village. In its place, solemn trepidation. It put Hans in mind of Londoners emerging after a bombing raid. Dolly remembered the tentative Kastany denizens, after the first pandemic lockdown finished.

CHAPTER 20

HANS and Dolly weathered the blizzard over to Froster, which was jammed with confused people taking comfort at the fireplace, huddling from attacks of nature and man. All, of course, talking about the shooting.

Merry hastened to her niece. She moved to embrace, but checked herself. 'Dolly, Hans, you're safe.'

'Yes, we thought he was coming for us. It was frightening,' Dolly said.

Taking them through the noisy throng to the last available table at the rear window, Merry told them that the bank had been robbed.

'Taffy's not around, he was down at base camp, apparently.'

Merry took their orders for more hot drinks. She was run off her feet and warned that it would take a while. The place was packed with excited *witnesses*, all talking at once. Hans got up and mingled, discussing his experience with anyone who would listen.

From her view at the back window, Dolly could see the trees thrashing, taking a beating from each other and throwing their detritus on the snow. Ice pellets peppered the window, like shrapnel. She wondered what Winston would make of it all and if he was safe in his bunker.

She listened to the recounting around her. Her table was bumped occasionally. A woman sat her bum on the back of Hans's chair. She heard one person tell how the robber was dressed all in white, with a white, fur-trimmed hood. Some said he fired his gun at people. Others said he fired it into the air.

Dolly heard many conflicting observations. She heard that the lone robber was a short man, a woman of medium height and a rather tall man. She heard that they threatened people verbally. She heard that they were silent throughout.

At the centre of most attention in the café was a young fellow who looked pale and shaky. He was the teller who had covered for Beth's departure and handed over the money at gunpoint. He answered questions slowly, wide-eyed.

Taffy's siren could be heard approaching the village. Dolly took all this in with a smile; she seemed strangely at peace.

After Taffy had taken the trembling bank teller to his office to make a statement, the crowd thinned out and Hans brought Dolly's parents to the table. Expecting to find her traumatised, they were surprised at the calm, confident manner in which she answered their questions and addressed their concerns. She seemed to pass it all off as just an adventure.

Jess worried. Merry brought them all drinks, while Dolly and Hans continued to relate details. Jess examined her daughter as she spoke, looking for signs that she might be masking the real effects. But she could see only the confident calmness.

'Taffy wants us to go over, later, to make a statement. There are detectives coming,' said Hans.

'Well, he can come to Innsbruck to do it,' said Jess, 'We'll get the commuter. We sent Carl and Maggie back, for safety. We didn't know what the hell was going on.'

Mark and Jess thanked Hans profusely for protecting their daughter and insisted he come to the lodge with them.

'We'll have lunch, relax, call Taffy from there.'

Barker rushed through the door as they were leaving.

'Are you alright?' he asked, with much concern.

Dolly smiled at him warmly.

'Yes, I'm fine, thanks,' she answered, touching his arm. *With a hint of affection*, Jess thought.

'We have to go, but can we catch up in the morning? Krumholz?' she asked.

'Yeah, sure,' he muttered, looking at Dolly's parents and appearing not entirely satisfied at being dismissed.

On the deck Jess asked, with a wry grin, 'Who was that?'

She expected irritation or dismissiveness from her daughter. Instead, Dolly looked at her openly, as an equal, and replied, 'Oh, that's Barker. He's a friend. The weather's better, blizzard's gone.'

***

Maggie and Carl ran at Dolly with a hundred cascading questions before she could hang her jacket in the drying room. But Jess herded everyone into the lounge, asking Carl and Maggie to go for more firewood. Hans settled in on the couch while Jess made lunch in the kitchen. Declining lunch, Klaus went up to his room and played a loud sonata.

Taffy was rather gruff when he arrived, explaining how his unusual absence from protecting the village was due to a stolen car found in a ditch at Base Camp.

Dolly's parents noted she communicated her account of

what happened in a measured, mature tone, appearing as if she was merely reporting lost property. Taffy informed her and Hans that detectives would arrive late and would want to speak to them in the morning.

As they saw him out, Dolly said, 'Goodbye, Mr Jones and thank you,' as if he had just dropped in with a plate of scones.

***

The following day, no matter how hard he tried, Barker could not get Dolly to talk much about her experience. She seemed dismissive of the seriousness of the incident.

'I wish I'd been there,' he said.

'Maybe you were. When you turned up at Froster would have been just enough time to ditch the white suit, bury the money and the gun.'

'You got me! What if I offer to split the dough?'

'Deal!' she said as they neared the end of the ride. Dolly began singing, 'Heartbeat, why do you miss when–' but she stopped and said, 'I was researching that World War One Christmas story Hans told us about.'

'Of course you did.'

'Reports are that, as well as singing and exchanging gifts, they actually played football.'

'Soccer, I suppose!'

'Yes. They actually played against each other in a friendly game.'

'Lucky it wasn't AFL or the truce might have ended badly,' Barker declared with a laugh, lifting the bar.

'I don't like to call it that,' she said, a little too sharply. 'That's another thing I would really miss if I did get to go to Europe,' she said, as they jumped off, sliding towards Wombat Run.

'What do you mean? What's wrong with calling it AFL?' he asked.

'If you play local basketball, they don't call it NBL. If you play soccer, they don't call it A-League.'

Barker shook his head, grinning. 'Does just about everything annoy you?'

'Not everything. Why can't we continue, as we did, calling it *Aussie Rules* or *Ozzer*? Yes. I'd like to call it *Ozzer*.'

'Okay, from now on it's *Ozzer*,' said Barker, taking off, his hands held up in surrender. He had been diverted again from discussion of the robbery and Dolly's dangerous experience. At Krumholz, Dolly ordered drinks and returned to their table in the sun.

'So, what did you *really* want to talk about?' he asked.

Unsteadily, she told him more about her 'mental health issues', her nightmares that morphed into waking-hour experiences and vice versa. It was a long, convoluted explanation, at the end of which, Barker merely smiled and said, 'We all have our demons, real and imagined.'

It was a fine, concise sentence from the electrical apprentice, reminding Dolly once again, not to be academically arrogant.

'Now, what's the Aurora problem you touched on? It seems to be a sore point,' he continued.

Dolly thought before answering. 'Yes, well, that's another problem.'

She explained how they were driving back from a visit to their grandma's in the country and continually encountered roadworks where the witches' hats were rolling around, scattered in the wind.

'Apparently, an *el cheapo* construction company had undercut all others to get some government and council contracts. They employed untrained staff and used cheap, imported stuff like the thin plastic, light-weight witches' hats.'

She explained how Carl came up with the idea of iron rings to sit over them, on the base, as ballast.

'The problem was how to sell the idea. Grandpa was prepared to make them, he's got a foundry, but we had to convince the works departments. That's where Aurora came in.'

'Who's Aurora?'

Dolly explained how the woman who appeared to be *maybe* hanging around with Uncle Lennie, seemed so nice and friendly at first.

'Carl and Maggie didn't warm to her, but she was unphased and started phoning the targets for us. She registered the business in her name because, like with Ziffers, we were under eighteen. But it was the phone calls that bothered me.'

'Why?'

'She told lies. She would say how she ran off the road with her children in the car because of the light-weight cones rolling around. Sometimes she said she'd hit a fence, various accidents and near-misses. It was dishonest.'

'Aren't all businesses a bit dishonest?' he asked.

'They don't *have* to be, we prove that with Ziffers.'

'Fair point.'

'She would call the same works managers a few times, pretending to be different women, with different stories, using different accents. Then she sent material promoting WitchRings.

'When she then phoned as a mother who had had a near-miss, threatening legal action, it was too much for me. I wanted out. Most councils put in orders; some ordered the contractor to buy them.'

'So, what's the big deal? Why don't you just leave her with it?'

'Because we control the website, the bookkeeping, the manufacture. If I tell Klaus, then it's all over.'

'So, why don't you?'

'Because she threatens to admit the fraud. She has evidence of our involvement from the start. She will take us down with her and ruin Grandpa's reputation, as well.'

'Does he know?'

'Klaus? No. He's very honest, he would be mortified.'

'Surely, she's bluffing.'

'I can't afford to risk it, but I've got to do something. Especially if I did get to go to Europe. I can't leave Carl and Maggie to deal with it, if it doesn't hit the fan soon, anyway.'

They caught the Cannonball chair with Imagine Dragons, taking them to the other side of the Summit, where Dolly knew it would be fairly unpopulated. Without a plan, or even a word, they took off down the slope together. She practised her slalom turns around imaginary gates and, to her surprise, Barker kept with her at times. She had never matched her skiing with a boarder before. Although Barker had to take a straighter line to keep up with her, they did many turns together, some of them beautifully coordinated.

At times, they crouched and extended in synchronicity, like expert dancers. On the lift, they laughed and discussed technique, good executions and near-tumbles.

They returned to Krumholz for lunch, where the sight of Justine-from-Trinity and her friends dining, did nothing to pale Dolly's flush of confidence. She noticed they looked over and whispered. She wondered if they were discussing her, or the handsome fellow she was with, or both. She wondered if they had spied and analysed her technique as Klaus had analysed Justine's. It was an unsettling feeling, having your movements, your particular nuances, monitored by a possibly superior competitor.

'Could you do me a special favour?' she asked Barker.

'Sure, what is it?'

'Could you go down to the carpark with me before the finals? We've got to get a large box of banners and cartons of Ziffers from my dad's car. Could do with some help.'

'So, you're going ahead with the prizes? You're not worried anymore?'

'I've grown up since then and we're doing banners, promotion, sales, as well.'

When Barker went off to the loo, Dolly's phone rang. She informed him on his return that she had to go to the police station with her parents and answer detectives' questions.

'You won't tell 'em it was me, will you?'

'No way,' said Dolly, laughing.

Chapter 21

On the walk back to the lodge, Mark, Jess and Dolly discussed the interview.

'Well, it's fairly certain that Roland's the bank robber,' said Mark.

'Yes, I think so,' said Dolly. 'It did look like his hunched posture driving the snowmobile. I'm reasonably sure it was him, but I wouldn't swear to it.'

'Their questions about Hans and Klaus,' said Jess, 'what was that all about?'

'They're covering all bases, I think,' said Mark, 'in case that Beth woman might have been in on it.'

Dolly wondered just how much adults knew, of which younger folk were ignorant.

'I suppose it is strange that she left right before the robbery,' said Dolly, 'but it's ridiculous to think men like Hans and Grandpa could have anything to do with a bank robbery.'

Mark and Jess exchanged knowing smiles and he said, 'Maybe not robbery. But a lot transpires under cover of darkness.'

'Best not to say anything to your grandfather, you know what a short fuse he has,' Jess added.

'Hans would have recognised Roland straight away, but apparently he had his head down the whole time, with a white face cover and there was the weather,' Dolly said.

'How are you feeling?' Jess asked her.

'I'm fine, it was an interesting experience.'

***

The next morning Dolly was seated on the deck at Froster. A number of students from her school had arrived at the mountain and Dolly noticed many of them heading to Heartbeat lift. A few gave a cursory wave, but most ignored her.

She usually wore her hair tied back, revealing the shaved sides, but this day she had let it down; the beautiful natural waves falling to below her jawline. She admired her reflection in the window and allowed herself to feel, well, *pleasing to the eye*.

'Nice hair,' said Barker, pulling up a chair. 'Is it a wig?' he added, laughing.

He quizzed her on details of the police investigation.

'I couldn't tell anyone that I had been to Tyrol before that. No offence, but I would have been in big trouble.'

Barker just smiled and said, 'None taken.'

'They asked a lot of questions about Beth. Clearly, she was the woman in white. Maybe I should have told them about her and Roland and how he threatened me. I was just scared Mum and Dad would go ballistic.'

'Rumour is, there were men other than Roland – including The Turk,' said Barker. 'Talk is, he left the mountain out of jealousy.'

'Anyway, the robber can't get far. You'd have to be pretty stupid robbing a bank up here. There's only one road off the mountain.'

'Yes, it does seem foolish.'

Just then, two girls called out to Dolly and hastened up the steps.

'Oh! Here come Schade 'n Freude,' she muttered to Barker.

'Dolly, hi.' But they weren't looking at her, as they sat down uninvited, smiling coquettishly at her companion.

'This is Barker, Barker, Jody and Nina.'

'I thought you said, Shay–'

Dolly stopped him with a kick under the table.

'Dolly, we heard you nearly got shot. How scary,' said Jody, grinning, unable to fake concern. Both classmates turned their attention back to Barker, with numerous inane questions. Dolly stood and ended the encounter as quickly as she could.

'Guys! We need to practice.' She ushered the girls towards Heartbeat. Clomping across the square, she noticed them glance back at the blonde-curled, good-looking dude she'd left behind.

'We saw that Justine bitch,' said Jody, on the chair.

'I don't think we need to call her a bitch,' said Dolly, 'she's just my competitor who might take the title and leave me with nothing to take to Europe, if I go, thereby ruining my life.'

'She and her friends are so arrogant, think they're better than everyone,' said Nina.

'The only thing to do is beat 'em,' said Dolly. 'Let's go over and look at the race area. I think we can practise beside it.'

Jody and Nina sang along to the Baby Animals' *Early Warning*, which played as they approached the top. Dolly rarely connected with her classmates – a decision that was usually mutual. She lamented being stuck with these two, especially. *Jody can't spell*, she thought, *and in texts, Nina uses 'there' instead of 'they're' and 'your' instead of 'you're'*.

The Interschools slope had been enlivened with colour, bunting and a large timber platform, with shelter and a kiosk for spectators. The track was complete, with starting box, gates and the finish line arch, all in place. The side slope was crowded, however. It seemed that most other students had the same idea. To make matters worse, there was Justine-from-Trinity ziffing smoothly, gracefully, with her *elite* friends. Dolly did two runs with her two fools, then retired to the platform to check the schedule of events. She was in the first heat that afternoon.

Returning to the race slope after lunch, Dolly shared the lift with Maggie, Carl and her mum. Mark and Klaus rode the chair behind. They understood they could only sell Ziffers the following day, at the semi-finals, when their product would be awarded as prizes.

'I don't see why we can't sell on finals day,' said Carl.

'Something to do with sponsors,' Jess answered. '*PAYING* sponsors.'

'We'll see,' said Carl, nudging Maggie.

One of the snow patrols passed below them with a rescue sled attached. It was the conveyance that the robber had abandoned somewhere near the carpark. The sled was always covered, so you could not tell if it was empty or carried a dead or injured body. Dolly leaned over the safety rail and watched it pass.

'I hope it's not a student in that thing.'

Justine-from-Trinity skied a beautiful run, with the fastest time. There were six more competitors before Dolly stood in the starting box.

On the platform, 100 metres below, she could make out

her excited, well-wishing family, waving. It was a heady experience. She thought of Justine's sleek race suit. She looked down at her old hand-me-down outfit. The rescue-sled was on her mind and she thought about the robbery. The bunting caused her to think of getting the Ziffer boxes from the car, with Barker. The starting gun sounded and she pushed off hard. She was happy with her technique around the first gate.

She remembered being accosted by Roland.

She chattered the second gate and slipped a little on the third.

Dolly then focussed on the task at hand. She negotiated the next few gates beautifully, perfectly, to the standard of her grandfather. Then she thought about Justine's one fault, which caused her to do the same. She refocussed again and finished the course commendably, recording the second fastest time. Behind *you-know-who.*

Dolly was furious. *Why can't you bloody well concentrate... focus?* she asked herself, looking up to the spectator platform. She could see her family and teacher clapping dutifully. She could not see Klaus.

Maggie noticed Dolly leave the area, skiing towards the bottom of Cannonball. She called to her brother to get his skis on and follow quickly. She knew how proud and pig-headed Dolly could be, that she was taking off so as not to have to face the questions or appraisal of others. While on the one hand, Dolly might want to be alone, Maggie thought she might also appreciate non-judgemental company.

'Don't say a word!' Dolly warned when they caught up with her at the Cannonball lift.

'I don't intend to,' said Maggie. 'I don't go to a private school. I don't give a stuff about your races.'

'Hmmph,' Dolly muttered and they boarded the lift where Dua Lipa sang 'Cold Heart' with Elton John.

Dolly did not want to talk, and her cousins felt it best to just maintain the silence. They tried to keep up with her angry runs down Drovers and Copperhead and across other remote slopes until Maggie was concerned they were almost in back-country. It was not foreign to Dolly, however. This is where she practised with Klaus. In her mind, she wanted to heal the faults, by revisiting his instructions, in the environment where they were imparted.

One run, however, was very long, with an almost flat trip across to where they could get another lift. Carl and Maggie were surprised to see Dolly waiting just through the trees. They stopped and had to step their skis carefully through, to join her. She was standing on the ridge above the igloos she had seen previously.

'So, this is where they are!' exclaimed Maggie.

The five igloos were positioned off to the side of a wide section of the Growler, where cross-country ski-campers would not be easily skittled by the dogsled.

'Turn your backs, ladies,' Carl announced, a tree separating him from the girls, 'I've got to pee off-piste.' He then proceeded to urinate down onto an igloo.

'X,' he said, trying to fashion the letter, 'marks the spot.'

'Carl! You're disgusting.'

'You dirty little pig!' said Dolly. Just then, she saw a quick movement at the entrance to the igloo.

'Someone's in there,' she whispered.

'Shit,' said Maggie and they started shuffling off without waiting for Carl.

It was hard work sliding and pushing along a mostly flat trail, until they reached a decent slope that got them to the bottom of Cannonball. Carl was admonished further when he caught up.

'When in nature, you've gotta answer the call,' he replied, grinning.

'Pity they didn't catch you at it,' said Dolly. 'Cross-country's finished, I thought,' she added, 'I didn't think there'd be anyone there.'

Dolly had placed high expectations on herself and was not looking forward to answering questions about her heat when they eventually made it across to Heartbeat and down to the village. She had arranged to meet her dad at Froster to get his car keys.

Chapter 22

'Yes! I had to invite *HIM*!' said Dolly, 'There are six cartons, three large, three small, plus the banner box. We needed some help.'

After a short wait, Barker joined them at the bus stop, where they caught the commuter down to the car park.

'How did you go in the race?' he asked.

'She did extremely well,' answered Maggie, a little too curtly, 'only a second off winning.'

He knew not to ask further.

They removed the cartons and stacked them beside the car and waited for the commuter to return. Dolly was explaining to Barker that her teacher had wangled the Ziffer prize deal, but she had been asked, as student and a competitor, to keep a low profile, to not be seen as promoting the business herself. While she was talking, Dolly noticed a huge pile of snow and wondered if it hid another car. She had time to kill, so she dug away with her gloved hand and, sure enough, uncovered a side window.

Just then, Leo walked over, dragging a shovel.

'I'd dig it out for you, but I don't really think it's yours,' he said with his crinkly-eyed, subtle smile. 'It's been there since the season started.'

Barker, Carl and Maggie had joined in scraping away at the snow.

'Hi, Leo,' said Barker.

Leo had a certain mystique at Dark Tower and was generally a loner who invoked curiosity. He merely saluted Barker with the shovel handle.

It soon became clear that it was a grey sedan. When Carl uncovered the Holden badge, Leo said, 'That looks like Roland's car.'

'Really? Are you sure?' asked Dolly.

'Pretty sure.'

'But why is it still here?'

'Well, I'm not the criminal type,' Leo answered, with a wink, 'but I would say he was clever and stole the car that was found in the ditch at Base Camp. He would've been easily spotted in his own car.'

At Dolly's request, Leo exchanged phone numbers, and said he would keep an eye on it.

'I'll let you know if this car leaves,' he said.

'Shouldn't we tell Taffy? Maggie asked.

'That's no fun!' said Leo. He and Dolly exchanged complicit grins.

On the commuter, Barker juggled a couple of cartons on his lap.

'It's a bit strange,' he said. 'I've had a bit to do with Roland and I never would have guessed he was that *criminal* or that *clever*.'

Maggie interrupted, 'I just realised,' she said, 'Taffy was already looking at the abandoned car at Base Camp while the robbery was in progress.' They discussed Roland's possible strategies. Dolly took in that Maggie and Carl forgot, at times, to treat Barker with disdain.

When the boxes were stacked in the entrance at Innsbruck, Barker declined Dolly's offer to come in. Before he left, Dolly asked them all to keep the *car business* to themselves.

'Please don't say anything to anyone. It might all be straightforward, but I want to think about it before Taffy gets involved.'

They agreed to keep their traps shut, and Barker took off to Dark Tower, where he expected to get at least a wink from Leo over his beer that night.

After dinner, the Ziffers discussed the events of the day, away from adults and Dolly fell to sleep easily, despite her race failure.

***

The next morning, as they climbed to the road, the kids found Klaus loading cartons of signage and Ziffer gaiters into the commuter. He stopped before boarding and said, 'Got some news. They will use Hester one more night to parade those VIPs, short ride around the village, then no more Jinker. Bit of a shame, though.'

'Do you know how she is?' Dolly asked.

'I had a good look at her. She's got a bit of a Suspensory Ligament Injury, in my opinion.'

'How do you know?' Maggie asked.

'You don't do farrier work for twenty years without becoming a bit of a vet.'

'Poor old John Thorpe will be out of a job,' said Dolly.

'Don't worry about Cliffy. I've offered him a job at the Anvil. Turns out he's done some shodding in his time. He can help Lenny while I'm up here.'

A little hesitantly, Dolly added, 'That's great news. I, er, wouldn't let him smoke there, would you?'

Klaus laughed. 'No. I did mention it. Nowhere near the Anvil, I told him. He'll be useful now Swaggy's moving on.'

'Swaggy?' Dolly almost shouted her question. She dropped her poles and her bottom jaw.

'Yeah. He was doing a bit for us. Left this morning to go walkabout again.'

Not understanding the stunned look on Dolly's face, Klaus got aboard and said, 'Good luck today, love.'

Down at Froster, Dolly sat alone on the deck, smiling to herself, barely able to contain her joy. One of her greatest horrors had just been erased. Leaving Yupik, Maggie and Carl shouted to her to *get going*. She raised her hand in a sign that asked for *just a little more time.*

Mark and Klaus were already setting up at the race site. It was agreed that Jess would sell, with a little help from Merry.

'I don't understand why I can't sell,' said Carl, as they rode the Heartbeat chair.

'Because you look like a young student, which contradicts Ms Rossi's instructions, and you'll be handling money, and you have the face of a criminal.'

'Fair enough.'

'Tell her your plan for Justine,' said Maggie. Turning to Dolly, she added with sarcasm, 'This will impress you.'

'I hand her a free Ziffer, tell her I was asked to by the lady, Jess, for her win yesterday. She wears it around arrogantly and, just before she races, I tell her the business and the gaiters, are owned by Dolly. It blows her elite-mindedness and she stuffs up her run.'

'You'll do well in corporate life,' said Dolly, sardonically, 'manipulating, hustling.' Carl still looked pleased with himself and Dolly added, 'When you're really large, you could lend money to poor Pacific nations, then demand fishing rights.'

Changing the subject, Carl said, 'I hope we sell a lot today and get a bag of cash.'

'I'm sure they have the card machine,' said Maggie.

Dolly reminded her that most students and a large percentage of skiers in general, carried cash because card readers failed, or did not exist, in the remote locales. 'That's why the bank stored so much cash.'

Jess had set up at one end of the spectator platform, cheerfully promoting Ziffers. Taffy was taking two mugs of coffee to a table nearby, to join Merry. *Making goo-goo eyes*, thought Maggie, sneering.

'I tried to call you,' Jess called out to Dolly, 'it was urgent.'

'Oh, my phone was still on silent. What was it?'

'I wanted you to drop in to see Lizzy on the way up. She has something for you, a present.'

'It can wait, can't it?'

'I suppose it will have to now.'

'Do you know what it is?' asked Dolly.

'No idea,' her mum answered, with a smile that said she knew perfectly well.

'Well, you can't go now,' said her dad, hearing as he came up behind her. 'You're the first skier in the first heat. You'd better get up there.'

Dolly stood in the starting box. She did not look at the spectators. She practised her relaxation shrugs and stretches. She was determined to be calm and concentrate.

The starting gun *cracked*.

Through the first half of the course, her technique was flawless; she was the embodiment of Klaus's precise instructions. *As opposed to Justine's sharper turns*, she thought – which caused her to unwittingly sharpen her turn on the next gate, then admonish herself – which caused a lack of concentration before the next and some adjustment before the one after.

Concentrate! she pleaded with herself. She completed the course in a time at least faster than the previous day.

There were many more competitors before Justine-from-Trinity, so Dolly waited on the platform, digging her fingernails into the railing and grinding her teeth. Her cousins strolled around, displaying Ziffer gaiters, and carrying posters. They caught much attention and sales were going well.

Competitors from the various schools mixed, laughed and generally enjoyed the occasion, without anxiety. Justine-from-Trinity and her two friends kept to themselves. They used a table off to the side of the platform, appearing to be planning their runs and analysing their competition. They did not wear Ziffers, of course, but instead, their usual white or mauve, expensive looking gaiters, bearing a fashionable logo.

It seemed to Dolly like an eternity, waiting for Justine's run.

Justine finished just 0.37 of a second slower and almost the entire platform erupted in congratulations for Dolly. Mark and Klaus ran to hug her. Aunt Merry seemed still too engaged with Taffy.

Dolly was buoyant skiing down to Little Envy with her cousins and, feeling like a whole day had passed, was surprised to find it was only 11.30 am.

Lizzy asked Carl and Maggie to sit and took Dolly to the back room. There she held a sleek, one-piece, green and gold, ski-race suit up against her and declared: 'Perfect. Exact size.'

'Wow! Is this for me?'

'Yep. It was Marje's when she was younger and slimmer. Try it on.'

It fitted perfectly. Dolly admired herself as best she could in the small mirror there and instantly allowed herself to feel much faster than Justine-from-Trinity.

'It's fabulous,' she said, running her hands down her sides and hips. 'Thank you so much. I love it.'

Carl and Maggie were equally impressed. Dolly strutted around the office while Lizzy made hot chocolates for them 'at the taxpayers' expense'.

'Thanks, again, Lizzy. I love it.'

'You're very welcome.'

The others finished their drinks, while Dolly perused the exhibits along the wall. Maggie noticed her mumbling as she read the Pygmy Possum poem.

She spoke the last lines aloud:

Avoiding their oblivian,

the fearful live subnivean.

She turned, looked at Maggie and Carl, then up at the shot-riddled, wooden duck.

'It's a decoy!' she said loudly.

'Yes,' said Lizzy, 'I *told* you it was a decoy.'

'No.' Dolly looked intently at Maggie. 'The car in the ditch, I think it's a decoy! What if Roland is still on the mountain? Then, in a few days, just drives off in his car without anyone noticing.'

Maggie took this in and asked, 'Then who drove the decoy?'

'Maybe it was Beth, or maybe it was Roland and Beth is the robber.'

'But where would he, or she, be hiding out in the meantime?' asked Lizzy.

'Subnivean!' said Dolly. 'In the igloo!' she exclaimed.

Turning to Lizzy, she said, 'Someone is in one of the igloos.'

'There shouldn't be anyone in any igloo,' said Lizzy. 'The school groups have finished and any cross-country skier has to get a permit from me to use them. No one has a permit, currently.'

'We were above them yesterday. I saw some sort of movement at an entrance of one.'

'That could have been a wombat,' said Lizzy.

'But what if it's not? We've got to check it out, Lizzy. What about the drone?'

Despite her government role, Lizzy had been up for a little scalliwaggery in the past. She had bent the rules a little but this was a bit too much.

'No. We should tell Taffy,' she said.

'That would spoil the adventure. You don't want to waste his time if it turns out to be a wombat.'

'The drone is worth thousands and it is government property,' said Lizzy.

'I'm sure we saw an Alpine dingo yesterday,' said Maggie. 'Didn't we, Carl?'

'I definitely saw it. Same area as the igloos,' Carl affirmed.

After a lot of pleading and arguing, Lizzy capitulated, against her better judgement. The Parks Department four-wheel-drive, with wheel chains jangling, headed off the main road below Dark Tower and took the Cattleman's Trail around the mountain. Lizzy doubted the dingo story, of course, and hoped no observer suspected misuse of government property, wishing to be seen with any passengers other than *these three*.

The track finished at a clearing, far along the Cauldron and the sky was still very clear. Lizzy set up her laptop on the bonnet, then the Ziffers helped her lift the drone from the back of the wagon. Once she guided the drone through the valley, tracing the course of the Growler, Lizzy was careful to avoid treetops, while focussing in on the igloos.

'I can't pan all of them without moving around trees,' she said. Watching the screen, they could see that she had a few near misses.

'Which igloo is it?'

'The third, I think,' said Maggie.

'The fourth, I reckon,' Dolly added.

'The one with a yellow X on top,' said Carl.

Dolly explained Carl's urinary graffiti effort.

'I think that's it,' said Lizzy. 'Fourth one, not yellow, but deep etching of a very messy attempt to make an X.'

'His handwriting is worse,' said Dolly.

Lizzy moved the drone back a little and lower.

'Something moved,' she said.

She piloted the drone to different angles from the entrance, all the time trying to avoid hitting trees. She tried to guide it further back, so as not to alert its inhabitant with the noise of the drone. But she had gone too close.

They all saw the figure emerge. Clad in the white outfit with the white, fur-trimmed hood, the figure raised a gun and fired at the drone.

'He's shooting!' Maggie yelled.

Trying to guide it back quickly, Lizzy hit some branches. She bucked and banked it. Two more shots were fired. Lizzy controlled the drone behind other treetops and further away, before turning for one more view. They saw the person clip into long cross-country skis, before turning and firing another shot, in vain, and pushing off down the Growler.

'He's going! I didn't know Roland could even ski,' said Maggie.

'That's not Roland,' said Dolly.

Lizzy guided the drone back to safety, and they loaded it, as quickly and carefully as they could, into the wagon. Despite objections from the Ziffers, Lizzy insisted on calling Taffy. But she had no phone service in that area. Taking bumps carefully, it was a slow trip back along the track. But, skiing the often-flat Growler, they knew it would be an equally slow trip to the car park, for the robber.

When they got to Little Envy, the Ziffers jumped out and grabbed their skis.

'Where are you going?' Lizzy shouted.

'To the car park,' Dolly answered.

'No, you're not! You wait here! I could be in enough trouble already. He's got a gun!'

But they took off, ignoring her loud pleas and warnings. Skiing hard down the side of Heartbeat and under Froster, Dolly and Maggie felt some trepidation, but the grin on Carl's face showed a fearless flight into dangerous excitement.

Lizzy got onto Taffy and told him what had happened. He was driving back up after meeting detectives at the abandoned car, at Base Camp.

'Stop... wait!' Dolly yelled, just beyond the village. She phoned Leo. She blurted the situation out too quickly, but he got the picture.

'That's handy. I'm at the car park now,' said Leo, laughing. 'Hang on.'

Dolly heard him yell, 'Hey, Matty, let me have the grader for a minute.'

After a long trek, some of it almost walking, the Ziffers *skrawwtched* to a stop above the car park and hid behind a pile of snow. From there, they had a view of the entrance. Dolly noticed Carl fashioning a tight snowball.

'You can't be serious! He's got a gun, idiot. Keep down.'

Dolly realised she had left the new ski suit at Little Envy and worried that Lizzy would be angry enough to take back the offer.

At that moment, they saw the car speed towards the entrance. Or, rather, it looked like a fast-moving snow-heap, as the robber had only had time to clear the windscreen. It took the corner onto the road too fast and, despite snow chains, it slid sideways a little, losing most of its load before straightening and accelerating. A loud *THGOOMP* left the driver seeing only white. The bonnet jammed under the top lip of the grader's bucket, and the pile of snow therein softened the impact, so that Leo felt only a slight jolt.

'Watch out, Leo, he's got a gun,' yelled Dolly.

'So have I,' declared Taffy loudly, pointing his police revolver at The Turk.

With all their attention on the escape, they had not noticed that Taffy had driven up the road, got out and already unholstered his pistol.

'Get out, slowly, turn and put your hands on top of the car.'

The other cop with Taffy handcuffed The Turk and put him in the back of the police wagon.

'Leo, thanks, mate. Well done.' Taffy grinned and waved to the Ziffers, taking the captive off to his office in the village.

Chapter 23

Dolly was poking the fire in the lounge room when her mum approached her. The others were in their rooms getting ready for another festival night in the square.

'The student exchange is back on again,' said Jess.

Dolly looked at her, surprised. Surprised because she did not know they had been off again, if Carl had lied, and surprised because her mother had raised the subject. And so warmly!

Jess smiled. 'It's been on-again, off-again, regularly. And, usually, I don't tell you. I know your heart is set on it – it'll probably break mine, but I need to let you grow.'

Dolly grinned and hugged her mum.

'You know, despite all the danger and excitement, I have slept well these past few nights.'

She knew her mum would still be concerned about the nightmares.

'I realised what a lot of the problem was. When Grandpa mentioned Swaggy, yesterday, I remembered I had seen clothes floating in the river and must have retained it in my subconscious. I think that's what caused murder and mayhem in my dreams. Combined with Shakespeare and war stories.'

It was a less-than-honest, sanitised version. Dolly felt a little ashamed being untruthful, but she wanted to take full advantage of her mum's current attitude.

'I feel I've matured a lot lately, a lot wiser,' she added.

Mark descended the stairs to witness his wife and daughter hugging.

***

The Village was again lit up with festival lights. Many people had gathered around the square to witness the VIPs arrive in the Jinker. A live band was setting up on a platform prepared near the Blarney. The familiar clinking and jangling could be heard approaching.

Then screaming and shouting rang out!

Maggie jumped up. Dolly froze; she had endured the robbery *and now, what's happening?*

Taffy ran from his office and others followed him to the track. The girls waited for a while on Froster's verandah, before deciding to go and investigate. But they had no sooner crossed the square when Mark, returning with most of the other spectators, approached, smiling. Herding the girls back to Froster, he said, 'The Jinker was attacked. Ollie Jacks was hurt.'

Seated back on the verandah, he told them that someone had ambushed the Jinker. The unknown assailant had hit Jacks in the head with a hard snowball, launched from a snowy knoll.

'He slumped onto his wife's shoulder, narrowly missed Emil and Maurie. They screamed and shouted.'

The development promotion speeches did not go ahead.

The band played a few tunes and was asked to pack up. Taffy marched across the square to his office, muttering and shaking his head.

People eventually wandered back to their various places around the village and Mark went off to the Blarney to join conversations about the attack. Maggie got hot drinks for Dolly and herself. When she returned, Dolly asked, 'Where's Carl? That attack could smell like his dirty work.'

'Wasn't him. He's washing pots out back.' Then she said, with some intensity, 'I've been eavesdropping.'

'That's dangerous,' said Dolly, smiling.

'Yeah, well, Grandpa was in Taffy's office. He was being asked about Beth. He said he hardly knew her, just to say *hello* and, get this, he stuck up for Hans! He called her Lady MacBeth and said Hans hardly knew her either!'

'That's weird. You just can't tell with people, can you?'

The girls went quiet when Jess approached. Lady Gaga's 'Stupid Love' could be heard from the Blarney's balcony. Dolly told her mum she was going up there to join Barker and his friends.

'They serve alcohol up there,' said Jess, 'I trust that you wouldn't drink. Those snowboarders don't drink, do they?'

'No more than real humans, Mum,' she replied, adding 'And no, they're not eighteen.'

On the balcony Glenn and Luke were smoking and drinking what looked like beer. The fire in the square sparked and flared, splashing a lightshow against the rock walls. The giant snowman, far from the fire, appeared fit and healthy.

Barker got up and walked to the end of the balcony to meet Dolly, where they leant on the handrail. He gave her an affectionate smile.

'I heard about the capture. And you were there!'

'Yes. It was quite exciting.'

'Wow. Why does everything happen when I'm not around?'

The fire-lit square below appeared to Dolly like a stage with footlights.

'Fire burn and cauldron bubble,' she murmured, as a fog began to infuse the village.

'Why the worried look?' he asked.

'Oh, I'm just concerned about bad weather rolling in. I've got my final tomorrow. I don't want the added burden of doing it in poor conditions.'

Taking in the cheerful patrons on decks, balconies and in doorways around the square, she said, 'It all seems now, surreal. I half expect them to be actors – Leo, Taffy, Roland, The Turk. They come out and take a bow and we all clap and cheer.'

The other Bandits let Barker know it was his shout and Dolly took in the scene below and beyond, smiling. She went over all the adversities in her mind and realised it had all left her with a real strength. She cringed internally, thinking of the child she had been so recently.

***

Roland was on a bus heading to Albury. Passengers might have noticed how he looked fondly at the older woman beside him. Clearly, it could be seen at times, he was infatuated. From her slightly bemused look and far-off gaze, however, it would also be clear, her thoughts were elsewhere.

Roland had driven the getaway snowmobile, with the gun-toting Turk hidden in the rescue sled. He attempted to discuss with Beth what they might do with their share of the money. But he was concerned about the vagueness in her responses. He tried to sleep, but his head knocked against the window as the bus lurched and rocked.

This was later remedied when he accepted a cup of coffee from Beth's thermal flask. He neglected to wonder why Beth did not drink also. She got off the bus in Albury and collected a black bag from the luggage-hold below. Roland would sleep all the way to Goonung, where detectives were waiting.

***

'What time's your race?' Barker asked when he returned with a full schooner.

'Eleven thirty. Finals for the other events are in the afternoon.'

'Can we go to Krumholz in the morning? I would like to talk without these clowns around.'

'Sure.' Then, nervously, 'What do you want to talk about?'

'Just stuff. Aurora, for instance. I've been thinking, there are laws against blackmail and the intimidation of minors. My Uncle Lawrence is a lawyer. I want you to talk to him. Won't cost you anything. I'll ask him, just a chat. Don't worry, I would never tell anyone else.'

Dolly paused for a moment.

'Let me think about it overnight. But, yes, meet at Krumholz.'

Maggie called out to Dolly from the square and beckoned her to come down. Carl was entertaining a group of young admirers with his embellished account of his role in the robber's capture.

'And then this almighty *THOOMP*, or *GROOMPH*... actually, I'm not sure what mat I pee on for that one!'

On Froster's deck, Taffy was entertaining Merry.

'They get up to mischief and I will pull them into line, but they're good kids.' Pointing to Carl, he added with a chuckle, 'Although I'm not too sure about that one.'

In a dream, that night, Dolly swam out fearlessly in a reedy lake to rescue a duck that was wounded with shotgun pellets. It was made of wood, but it quacked feebly in pain as she nursed it back to shore. She woke feeling calm and refreshed.

CHAPTER 24

BETH was heading inland, along the Murray, in a silver Peugeot. She had satisfactorily conned The Turk, manipulated Roland and flirted with Hans, Klaus, and even Taffy, to gain village information. She took one hand from the steering wheel and flipped open the bag on the passenger seat, smiling at the large horde of cash.

***

Dolly dropped off a cake, that Merry had baked, to Lizzy, thanking her once again for the ski suit. She wanted to get to Krumholz as soon as possible, but Lizzy was inconveniently talkative. She asked about the robbery and fired numerous questions that Dolly answered with unsatisfactory detail. Then she touched on the Jinker attack, where she and Marje were supposed to be seated, originally, with Jacks and his wife.

She examined Dolly's face as she spoke. Unsure of the innocent positions of the Ziffers, she wondered if they might be responsible, after what she had overheard the other night at Innsbruck. She detected no guilt, however, and thanked her for the cake. Lizzy could see she was keen to get away and wished her good luck in the final as she bolted out the door.

Dolly got across to Blue Shoulder lift and skied down to Krumholz. The café sheltered in a copse of blizzard-beaten snow gums, gnarled and twisted like old folks' limbs, exposed to the worst weather that came up the valley. But this was a friendly morning with a clear sky.

Dolly planted her skis upright in the snow and, stepping onto the deck, admired her new, sleek, form in the full-length window, as she walked. She waved to Henry, the owner, and found Barker on the crowded verandah, enjoying the sunshine.

'Wow, look at you.'

'You like it? Just hope it gives me an edge. I *am* a bit nervous.'

Barker offered to get drinks and Dolly opted for a strong, hot, coffee. When he returned, he said, 'I've gotta tell you something, those guys you saw us roughing up the other night...' Dolly was poised for a moral dilemma, but Barker explained that the two Interschools snowboarders were the ones who had thrown the snowball that injured Hester.

'So, do you think it was them again last night? she asked.

'No. It wasn't.'

'Who did it, then? Hell, Hester could have had another fall. That would.ve been the end of her. Do you know who did it?'

'No. I don't,' he replied. 'I have vague suspicions it was some older gentlemen, but, as no horse was harmed, I think we'll leave it there.'

Dolly eyed him, suspiciously.

'If I was to ask you who would be the most vocal critics of further resort development amongst the folk at Tyrol–'

Barker rubbed his chin, feigning ponderance.

'I'd have to say Leo and the other shovelers and my dad.'

Dolly changed the subject and they went over the events of their current snow season. They talked about the fixture of football games they would be playing when they got back and how they could organise to catch up.

'I'd like to take up your offer to speak to your uncle,' she said, 'I'll take Mum or Dad along. I'm going to tell them all about Aurora.'

'I think that's a good idea.'

'I have to show them I've matured,' she said, chuckling. 'The pandemic restrictions have eased in Europe and that monster appears to be limiting his vile atrocities to the poor people of Ukraine. I think they'll let me go.' At this, Barker was merely pensive. 'I must expand my education and explore the opportunities.'

'Well, Ziffers won't make your fortune, from what you tell me,' said Barker, pretending ambivalence, 'and WitchRings have had their day. You might as well become a professor.'

On the Summit lift, Dolly looked at the time and realised she had *Dolly-dallied* too long. Barker asked if he should come and cheer her on.

'No,' she told him, 'go and join your friends, I'll catch you later.'

On a ridge out of sight of the race slope, they stood side-by-side, skis and snowboard pointing in opposite directions. Dolly put a hand to Barker's helmet and pulled his face to hers. She kissed him! On the lips! For four seconds! The usually cool Kelvin grinned goofishly.

Dolly smiled and skied off. For her first kiss, she had taken the bull by the horns. She experienced a slight euphoria, like one of those snowflakes that tease gravity, fluttering and dancing down. It was time to face life the same way.

At the platform, Ms Rossi, informed her, 'There's only one before you, after the next, *so get up there.*'

She caught the lift, alighting to Kingswood's 'Bitter Sweet' and skied down to the start.

Justine-from-Trinity was there.

'Hi, Dolly, we haven't met. I'm Justine.'

'Nice to meet you, finally,' said Dolly, taken aback by her competitor's good nature. There was not a hint of animosity. Her face bore a genuine, open smile. The gaiter was scrunched around her neck, but Dolly could make out the distinctive 'Z' logo.

'You skied well yesterday,' Justine said. 'You didn't need to win the Ziffer, I'm told. I did a personal best, myself.'

'Well done,' said Dolly. 'Good luck, today. Break a leg.'

They both laughed. And, with a natural cheerfulness, Justine took off as the gun *cracked*. Dolly stood at the starting line and looked out, beyond the course, across the low-lying clouds. Her vision was beyond the wide brown land, spanning the seas, to Europe. She imagined the glacier in Norway. She felt herself ziffing through life now.

Without watching down, she imagined that Justine would make the same small errors that would slow her a little. Justine, who didn't take it too seriously, as it turns out, would just enjoy what she was doing.

Dolly took on a calm confidence in her green and gold suit. She cleared her mind, smiled, relaxed, and determined her perfect run.

The gun sounded. She pushed off, and down, to her future.

Shawline Publishing Group Pty Ltd
www.shawlinepublishing.com.au

Milton Keynes UK
Ingram Content Group UK Ltd.
UKHW020700280824
447448UK00010B/147